A
Harlequin
Romance

SMUGGLED LOVE

by

DORIS E. SMITH

Harlequin Books

TORONTO • LONDON • NEW YORK • AMSTERDAM • SYDNEY • WINNIPEG

Original hardcover edition published in 1976
by Mills & Boon Limited

ISBN 0-373-01992-0

Harlequin edition published July 1976

For Sidney and Muriel
In gratitude

Printed in Canada

CHAPTER ONE

OUR Boeing flew in low over the sea. It skimmed the coast, the rock pools and the black and white cattle. I wished I could have caught those last gold drops of the sun on the little fields below us, but there was no time. We had landed. We trundled in past a jumbo jet and stopped. Someone reached me the kangaroo from the coat rack. It had attracted attention at Heathrow and was still doing so as I heaved it under my arm with its false eyelashes down and its velvet bottom up. Half an hour later I was in the coach that was waiting to take us to the city.

The driver had native wit. As he worked his way down the aisle collecting fares man after man handed him a pound note. The middle-aged lady sharing the seat with me had the exact amount ready in coin. He took it gratefully, announcing: 'The girls are the best!'

'Now I know I'm in Ireland,' she said to me with a smile.

The long, long journey had not gelled for me till that moment. I too was in Ireland. The moment had arrived. I was home.

The ice had been broken and my companion chatted to me as the coach moved on through the vast new precincts of the airport. Was I a visitor? If so, could she help?

'No necessity, thanks,' I said, laughing. 'I'm a native!'

'Oh, for goodness' sake, I'd just decided you were Swedish!' she admitted frankly.

It was not the first time that had been said to me. Traditionally I should have been dark or red-haired. I wasn't. I was pale blonde with green eyes and bumpy cheekbones. My name was Judith Mary Gale, I was rising twenty-five and I was broke. I had had to sell practically all I'd got to bring me here. You don't get an air ticket from Sydney to Dublin for peanuts.

I had been away for four years, not all of them spent in Australia. My seat-sharer was a total stranger, but she

5

had a friendly face, and I needed that. I had come through the swing door from Customs into the Arrivals area feeling as though I were sleepwalking. Faces had turned as faces always do in such circumstances, but the days when one particular and dear face would loom out of the crowd for me were gone. My mother's sudden death from a coronary thrombosis two months ago had been like a buttoned foil until this moment. Now the point was naked and twisting my guts.

So I talked. Quickly and breathlessly. Hardly letting my kindly companion get a word in.

Three years at the School of Art and Design had convinced me that I wanted more, more classes with different teachers, more experience, above all new horizons. So off I had gone from Dunbeagle, the village in Meath where my father was a G.P., first to London, then to Edinburgh and next to Toronto. I learned to type and kept myself by taking office jobs. Any time I had to myself went in attending art classes and in sketching. The world hadn't come to my feet, but my stuff sold and the day when it might even support me drew nearer.

My parents approved my efforts and had never held me back, but would I ever forgive myself for that cancelled holiday? A year ago when all my plans were made to go home, the company for whom I was working in Toronto had offered me the chance to transfer, passage paid, to Sydney. Australia, New Zealand and Japan were future objectives, but it would have taken years to save up for the fare. So instead of going home I had flown on to Sydney, and it was there two months ago that the news about Mother had come to me.

There had been no question of going home for the funeral. I hadn't that kind of money and Dad had managed to reassure me at the time that there was no need to worry about him. But as the weeks went by I did worry, so somehow I'd raised the fare with a bit of help from the company's benevolent fund, and here I was.

My new acquaintance endorsed my action warmly. 'I'm sure your father has been counting the days to see you.'

'Oh no! I haven't told him,' I laughed. 'I know him of

old. He wouldn't have let me come.'

'So you took no chances,' she commented. 'I think that's wonderful. Good luck.'

There was nothing wonderful about it. I didn't delude myself. I had done this quite as much for my own sake as for Dad's.

Dunbeagle was no great distance from Dublin, but I had to wait for the bus. As I sat in the station, I was a child again coming home for the holidays in my hard straw boater, and counting the hours till we would get to the gates of Haresmead. Mummy would let me out of the car and drive on home and I would pelt up the overgrown drive and burst into Hew Trelawney's cottage. 'Hew, Hew, where are you? I'm back!'

Hew always had time and was never stumped by my questions. He could pick out a horse's hoof and enlighten me on the habits of badgers, and he could paint. Oh, the treasure house that dusty untidy cottage was to me! I spent hours in it, rummaging through Hew's stack of canvases, watching him work and producing my own first messy masterpieces.

The cold tap dripped merrily into his sink, but that was part of the joke. Not worth bothering, Hew would say, he had only come for six months two years ago.

The place to which he had come was also magical. It was Haresmead, once the big house of Dunbeagle, now shuttered and empty, a place of dreams. Its owners were English and though my father could remember the days when they used to come over for the hunting none of the present generation had ever been near the place. It had been closed up for two years or more, a prey to damp and bindweed, when one day Hew had got off the bus in the village and explained that he had been given the job of caretaker. Wages in kind, he had announced cheerfully, the free tenancy of one of the lodges on the estate. In days, not weeks, his long gangling figure had found its niche.

He was unashamedly shabby with clothes that I once heard Mummy say 'you could spit through'. He cut his hair himself, straight round in a bob, and he was as thin as a rake. I thought it dreadful that the rich owners of Hares-

7

mead had not put a bathroom into the lodge, but Hew seemed quite happy with a hip bath in front of the kitchen fire. He kept this piece of equipment standing against the wall and it used to fascinate me. He must, I thought, get into it in sections!

For months I had not been able to bear my memories, but now in some strange way they didn't hurt so much. I sat there with my arms full of kangaroo and my legs stowed neatly between my suitcases, dreaming of other days.

Odd how some days stick in your memory and have a kind of colour.

That day in 1964 as we drove home from the meet trailing the horsebox with Prince inside there were pink bars in the sky and the country was red with berries. We had been out with one of the hunts to which my father belonged. I, through the kindness of Hew who owned Prince but gave me sole rights to him in the holidays.

Nothing turned my father on like the hunt, but general practitioners don't have much spare time and he got a poor enough return for his two memberships, the local staghounds and the foxhounds whose terrain lay to the south. Hew didn't belong to either, though he kept two horses in the old stables and taught me a lot about them. If I should have questioned the fact that he had bought Prince, a Hafflinger pony who was too small for him but just my size, I never did. Life was too good.

Dad often teased me about the amount of time I spent with Hew, and after we had got in from the meet and had had the usual scrimmage for the bathroom he pounded jokingly on the door and told me that the sooner I took Hew to the altar the better.

Mummy was organizing a charity cheese and wine party that evening in the parish hall and later when I was dressing she came to my room. I remember my party gear, a lacy white blouse and a red velvet pinafore, and I remember tugging my hair out of its ponytail and combing it over my shoulders. Mummy had stood there looking as though she didn't know where to begin.

'Ju darling,' she said at last. 'You mustn't take too

much notice of Daddy. You know how he pulls people's legs. Hew is a very nice man, but he's much older than you and you mustn't be silly about him.'

What was this? First I was bewildered, then angry.

'Ju, look in the glass, pet,' my mother had urged unexpectedly.

She had come over, resting her hands on my shoulders, and there we both were, reflected in my white-framed mirror. My hair was like long yellow satin, Mummy's was brushed up and burnished; my eyes were smooth and naked, a map pen had drawn in the tiny lines round hers and she was wearing pale green eyeshadow. But we were very alike.

'Do you see what I see?' she asked softly, and pressed her hand on my shoulder. 'You're very pretty, darling. It has to be paid for.'

'Then I don't want it.' I said stormily.

'Oh, you will, Judy,' Mummy said gently. 'You will.'

The bus to Dunbeagle had now drawn into its stance and I got aboard. Soon we were off again inching west through the evening traffic along the quays. This part of Dublin had not changed, the wide grey waters of the Liffey slapped indolently against the quay walls, pedestrians thinking of home passed each other on the arc of the 'Ha'penny Bridge'.

I had not seen as much of home in the years that followed my fourteenth birthday. The school took parties of us abroad in the holidays and we all took jobs during the long summer break. Inevitably I also saw less of Hew. But during the autumn term of my last school year Mummy mentioned in a letter that he had had 'flu and Daddy was concerned about the cottage, which was damp.

It was ages since I had written to Hew. At one time we had kept up a correspondence and I had passed his letters with their delightful thumbnail sketches of Prince round all my form, but gradually it had died. Now I was stirred and anxious. I wrote warmly urging him to take care of himself and promising that I would be up to see him the moment I set foot in Dunbeagle for the Christmas holidays.

9

Hew sent me back a charming letter, assuring me that he was 'restored' but adding that he would welcome moral support. 'Young Martin, the bright boy of the family' was coming to stay over Christmas and it would be 'a case of look out for squalls, not to say more positive expressions of disapproval'. There followed a drawing of a long figure with 'H' on the pocket of his pyjamas staring wrathfully at an apple pie bed.

I had not known Hew had a schoolboy relation, but no matter about that. It was a call to arms. No precocious brat should cheek Hew while I was around.

There had followed Christmas 1967 – of horrendous memory.

Could my thoughts help going back? The bus had now left the city behind and the Liffey had become a pleasure river, its banks marked by the club houses and craft of the various rowing clubs who used it. In a few moments we would run into the village of Chapelizod. 'But where *are* the lizards?' I had once asked disappointedly as we drove over the bridge.

There were no lizards. The name was not 'Chapel-lizard', they explained, but Chapel Iseult; if you wanted the more usual version of the name 'Chapel Isolde'.

That Christmas, 1967, Isolde and I had stood face to face.

It was a cold bright morning, my first in Dunbeagle and every muddy rut trapped a split of silver. I thrust the ends of my jeans into my boots and ploughed along.

My parents had not been able to fill me in on 'young Martin'. Daddy had not seen Hew since his final visit to the surgery, Mummy had meant to look him up but had herself had 'flu. She had, however, made him a plum pudding and I had it with me.

'You're very fond of him, aren't you?' she commented as I set out.

I was. I had no special boy-friend. Somehow none of the boys I knew – and at school we mingled regularly with the neighbouring boys' college – really interested me. That was all right, because I was going to be much too busy for the next few years to cope with a conflict of interest.

'Well,' Mummy said indefinitely, 'he's a dear soul and I know I can trust you both.'

'We are *not* talking about the same thing,' I told her. 'I may never marry.'

'Come back to me when you're twenty-five,' she retorted.

Neither of us at that moment could look ahead; it was merciful.

There were many roads to Haresmead. I took a bridle path which began at the back of the churchyard and must have been made by past generations from the big house wending their way to church. A rusty gate led out on to the hillside and I squelched through the gorse and heather, pausing often to enjoy the view. The strong wind that whipped my hair out behind me seemed to clean all the colours. The sky was a clear bright blue, the grass in the graveyard emerald, the gorse that, like kissing, never went out of season was pure gold.

The first landscape I had ever attempted was this one, but try as I would the message I was after – the flying hill and the graves sleeping below it – eluded me time and again.

Hew's lodge in the woods was grey with arched windows. He drew back the bolts on the door every morning and did not secure them again till he was going to bed. I loved that about him, his trust and his welcome.

'It's me, Hew!' I called happily. 'Where are you?'

There was no answer, so I did the obvious thing, put my hand to the kitchen door and pushed. Warmth and the smell of breakfast wafted out. You could find anything in Hew's kitchen, from stray animals to . . .

I felt as though I had been shot.

'*Out!*' it commanded again as I turned.

'*Get* out!' a voice exploded.

Ye gods! There was a man in the bath. In the second before I backed out and closed the door he seemed to be very dark. I had caught a glimpse of brown shoulders and white soap trails. The face was a kind of blur, but there had been a round mouth and shooting dark eyes. Very angry, I realized feebly, as I supposed he had every right to be.

The pity of it was that in the circumstances I couldn't stay and give my side of it. I had been in and out of Hew's cottage for four years and he *never* took his bath in the morning.

Hew sloping up the ride at that moment was a welcome sight, though I had to admit his appearance gave me a shock. He was thinner than ever and when the gale lifted his hair, the skin beneath it was white and almost transparent. But he was the same old Hew, hugging me with long arms to his shabby pullover.

'Judy, me old segocia, welcome home! You do these old eyes good.'

'Segocia' is a funny word that no two people spell the same way but which everyone knows is a special Dublin endearment.

'You're thin,' I said distressfully. 'Did Daddy give you a tonic?'

'His best,' Hew answered. 'The one he put down seventeen years ago. Come on, let's get in the warm.' He linked my arm and frowned when I drew back. 'What's the matter? Aren't you coming in?'

'Not now!' I said decisively. 'If there's one thing I don't really need it's being shouted at by a strange man in a bath.'

'Oh, crumbs.' Hew looked guilty. *'You've been in?'*

I nodded silently.

'In the bath, you said?' he repeated still hesitantly.

'In front of the fire. Splashing himself,' I said with venom. 'And he didn't like me much.'

'He wouldn't. He hasn't much sense of humour,' Hew returned gloomily. 'But don't worry, shipmate. I'm sure you'll never see as much of him again!'

It was a certainty I thought of the bright angry eyes and the brown drawn up knees. That bath had always been ridiculous.

'I'm not going to see any of him again,' I amended. 'When is he leaving? When do you expect your Martin?' Hew, thank goodness, had only one spare bed.

He was looking at me, I realized, with a studiously casual face. 'Oh, I should say, as soon as he's got some clothes on.'

Hew thought it a joke that I should have concluded that Martin was a schoolboy. 'Purely symbolical,' he said lightly when I referred him to his drawing of an apple pie bed. 'He'd turn this place upside down if he could – and me with it. My cousin is a man with a mission. He disapproves of me. Come, let's go and meet him.'

There was no sign of Martin when my reluctant feet took me back over the threshold of the kitchen. The empty tub was there and Hew murmured that he hoped the baby had not been thrown out with the bath water. There was no such luck. A few moments later the door opened.

Dressed in smart checked trousers and a high dark sweater, Martin Trelawney was every bit as indelible as before. The word was Gallic. Short black hair waving slightly at the temples, dark brown eyes, olive skin. I wish I need not say this, because I didn't like him, but he was plain gorgeous.

Hew introduced us with a flourish. 'Judy, Martin Trelawney, the family tycoon. Martin, Judith Mary Gale, the love of my life.'

Somehow even then, without anything that happened later, I felt the flash of enmity. I say 'enmity' for want of a better word. Perhaps 'awareness' would be more correct. At all events, I felt as though I were under a microscope and Hew with me. Martin Trelawney looked from one to the other of us in a silence that seemed to last for minutes.

'Coffee,' Hew said gaily, bustling round. 'Coffee for two, breakfast for one. Sit you down, Martin. And the blame is mine, so don't look at Judy like that. It's not her fault you can't lock the door.'

'Was I looking at you, Miss Gale?' Martin asked coldly. 'In that case I apologize.' Despite his warm colouring I had seldom seen such an icy glance.

'I suppose I should also apologize to you,' I began clumsily.

'There's no compulsion,' he said offhandedly, picking up the sugar bowl and giving its mended lid a closer look.

From that moment I knew that the holidays were doomed.

'Cheer up.' Hew had been watching my face. 'His bark is worse than his bite and even if he is too big for Ludo I'm sure he'll let you play with his soldiers!' He actually managed to look at his guest with affection.

'I doubt if Miss Gale would find war games particularly diverting,' Martin returned smoothly.

'I think she'd enjoy seeing your models,' Hew disagreed mildly. 'I did tell you art is Judy's field.'

Martin looked at me indulgently. 'And a wide one,' he pointed out politely. 'In which it is possible we would find ourselves at opposite corners. My art must pay for its keep. That's the criterion. Will it sell?'

'That's all right if you just want to be commercial.' I knew he had programmed me straightaway. *Long hair – jeans – muddy boots – will end up living off her father.* That was the last thing I would do. But you had to be true. You couldn't degrade your gift.

'Indeed I do,' he returned promptly.

'At the expense of merit?'

'I wouldn't say that. I'm sure you could sell the Mona Lisa.' He scrunched a piece of toast.

It was a relief when Hew turned the conversation by asking if I wanted Prince for the meet tomorrow. I said: 'Yes, *please*, if he's ready,' and we went round to the stables so that I could see for myself.

Hew was not the most methodical person, but he certainly made an exception in the care he lavished on that Austrian pony. Getting a horse fit for hunting demands a planned régime of diet and exercises, and when there is only one man and two horses it is hard work. In fact, Hew's big horse, Black Eagle, was not being hunted this season, he was not in good enough shape. But Prince, as always, was waiting for me in the pink of condition.

Now as the red and white bus carried me towards Dunbeagle all the people from that Christmas came out to meet me.

Mummy's reaction when I told her about Martin had been typical. She gave a party for him the very next night. It was a last-minute affair with invitations by telephone, but everyone accepted.

Mummy's parties were always successful. For openers,

they had a good setting. Our house is nice and old and looks super with log fires. I was handing round dishes of nuts and sticks of pineapple and cheese when one of the guests who had gone out to check his headlights came back looking slightly glazed. 'This cousin of Hew's, what did you say he did?'

When I shook my head he conducted me to the window and lifted a fold of curtain. I put down the pineapple sticks and said: 'Crikey!'

The modest family saloons parked in our drive had been joined by a sports coupé so widely winged that it looked as though it might fly. Hew and Martin were walking away from it. It began to dawn on me then that Hew's jests had been half truths, for if ever I had seen a car for the road to the boardroom that was one.

Martin seemed to enjoy the party and I discovered that he could smile. He was not over tall, but he had very straight shoulders and his charcoal-grey striped suit made the most of them. Where all the other men had white shirts, his had a brown stripe and he had black and brown in his tie. The funny thing is that I can see him still, standing there with a pineapple stick in one hand and a glass in the other. He had small hands and the backs of them were golden brown.

Someone came along at that point and asked me about the day's hunting. Foxes were rampant just then both in Meath and Kildare. We had seen three, two had got away. Then the last covert had been drawn and a third one had emerged and made for the canal. He had swum it twice, across and back again with the pack after him and when he had landed on the bank the second time a hound who had stayed behind had got him. It had been over in a flash and the huntsman who was friendly with my father had given me the brush.

At this point I found myself talking quickly and conscious that Martin had come over and was staring at me.

It was a desperately private area, I never showed it even to myself for more than a second. I had a rule: 'Don't be sorry. A fox is bad, but a dog would be frightful and a horse – unbearable.'

In the week after Christmas Martin Trelawney really made his mark in Duneagle. He borrowed brushes and cleaned the cottage chimneys, made a bonfire of all the old newspapers Hew had been hoarding and found some-one to scrub the floors. After this we were invited to supper.

I couldn't remember when I had last been in Hew's sitting-room because he never used it except as a dumping ground for paintings. Now it was clean and tidy and warm and because I could always read Mummy's mind I knew she was thinking of offering new curtains.

Martin had his coat off and was cooking supper.

'I tell myself,' Hew murmured whimsically, 'that if I don't look at him he'll go away.'

The words were mild, but they went to my heart. Hew was an artist, you must make some allowance for un-tidiness.

'Untidiness, did you say?' Martin challenged. 'Not only that. The place was a fire-trap.'

Perhaps so. Indeed my father had already said as much, but surely the situation could have been handled with more tact?

For supper we had stuffed tomatoes, bacon fried with apple and little balls of cheese and olive, and everything was done to a turn. When the meal was over we sat round the fire, Hew brought out an old guitar and Martin rattled off with a spiritual.

'*Dust, dust and ashes are flying o'er my grave,*
But the Lord shall take my spirit home.'

Music is a liberating thing. Much as I disliked Martin Trelawney, I couldn't stop my hands clapping the beat. And picture number three went into my gallery – brown shirt, lemon tie, and an eyelid drooping suddenly into a wink.

We learned that he had come down from Cambridge a year ago with a Bachelor of Commerce degree and was now a management trainee with a giant group in Staffordshire. One of his interests, already hinted at, was war games. He fetched two of his model soldiers to show

Dad – a Prussian knight and a Persian warrior from the time of Darius.

I don't know what I had expected, but certainly nothing so delicate or perfect. Darius's foot soldier was half the size of my little finger, but the detail was needle-sharp, black hair brushed from a skull cap, chiselled profile, pointed black beard. He carried his bow and quiver on his back.

The Prussian was bigger and on horseback. His helmet was gold and he wore a leopardskin over his armour. A feature was his 'wings', originally made from eagle feathers mounted on slats. Everything had been lovingly reproduced in the model, even to the fluttering red pennon on the tiny lance.

Martin volunteered that he bought the lead castings, but did his own assembling and painting. The Prussian, just finished, was the pride of his collection and needed careful handling. 'Mind him, please,' he warned as I took the model into my hand. 'He's twenty-five millimetre and if you dropped him he'd break. That's because of his weight.'

The night was the nearest I had come to liking Martin, though on the way home I remember squabbling with my father about him.

'That lad's a doer,' Dad had pronounced. 'He'll go places.'

'Like a juggernaut!' I had retorted. 'What I'm wondering is what's Hew got that he wants?'

'I'll tell you one thing,' my mother said, turning her head. 'Prince.' She pointed out that it should have struck us before. With Black Eagle out of commission and it going without saying, as always, that the pony was my property in the holidays, Martin had never had a ride at all. And he *was* a horseman. Those friends he had mentioned staying with had a riding stables in Wiltshire.

'Oh, what a bore!' I said disgustedly.

Old as I was, I could have cried. There were still two meets scheduled before I went back to school and I had counted on going to them. Surely, I thought childishly, Hew would not hear of my standing down.

Alas, he accepted my offer, carefully avoiding my face

which had dropped about half a yard.

A day or so later I went up to Haresmead. The fox-hounds were meeting three miles away and my father had taken the afternoon off to go with them. He always hired a horse for the season and he'd offered to get one for me, but I had said no. Hiring was not cheap and I'd had my whack of hunting for these holidays.

I went to Haresmead because I thought Martin would have gone to the meet. The conclusion, however, was faulty. As soon as I opened the cottage door, I heard his voice: 'Well, what's the verdict? Any good?'

There was someone with him, a prosperous-looking middle-aged man at that moment polishing his spectacles with a large white handkerchief. Beside them, ranged along two walls of the kitchen, was a selection of Hew's paintings. All were familiar. There were landscapes of Dunbeagle, animal studies mostly of Eagle and Prince and a set of watercolours featuring me. These had been done three years ago, four head and shoulders portraits each one of which showed me wearing different headgear.

A second served to show me what was happening. The stranger had put on his polished glasses and was standing back. The astuteness of his gaze made me hot. Hew and I had always been so close that it was almost like having my own work assessed. There were many years between us, but something uncertain about his smile always made me want to protect him.

So I stood there in the doorway glowering and suspicious.

In the same instant Martin spotted me. 'Not again?' he remarked teasingly. 'You really have a genius for seizing the moment.'

It confirmed my fears that something was being hatched.

'Is Hew around?' I asked.

From the way Martin said: 'No, he's gone up to Dublin,' I knew that this too was part of the plan.

Hew's paintings were being vetted behind his back. It was infamous!

'What's happening?' I jerked.

'I'll tell you,' Martin drawled smoothly. 'You've left

the door open and it's hard enough to keep this place warm without that. Close it and come in. You may learn something.'

Of all the cheek! I wished for the moral fibre to walk away, but despite my indignation I was intrigued and dying to hear the expert's opinion.

He was not so unprofessional as to oblige. The owner of an art gallery in Dublin – his name had been given to Martin by mutual friends – he was a man of few words and little could be judged from his expression as he went down each line of pictures. Disappointingly, neither Eagle nor Prince seemed to register. He smiled when he came to my four hats and gave me a look of recognition. In fact he stood longest at 'Great-Granny', which was what we always called the picture in which I was wearing an old-fashioned straw hat with a lot of flowers on the brim.

'Pleasant,' he said at last.

Why was Martin doing this? I questioned resentfully. Hew was such a private person and painted so much of himself into his pictures that I felt we were trespassing.

'There's one more I'd like you to see,' Martin was telling the connoisseur. 'It's the test case,' he added, opening the door of the cottage.

I was mystified as I followed across the clearing on to the main drive and up to the house.

This had once been the most exciting place I had ever known, now it was the saddest. As a dreamy child, and looking back on myself, I was ashamed to own how romantic and unsophisticated I had been, it was the key to all my imaginings. At night the witches rode around its chimneys and a headless horseman drove his ghostly team up the avenue; by day I peopled it with a sleeping princess and the prince who would come and wake her with a kiss. But now I saw only an empty house that no one cared about. The broken glass in the beautiful half-moon fanlight gave me a lump in the throat. Lovely to think that some day it would be restored to its former grace but only a pipe dream. Hew's job went no further than a watchdog. He was never given authority to effect repairs.

Be that as it may, however, he kept the key on his

person and I didn't see how Martin hoped to effect entry. To my horror, he took off his coat and broke in. There were no catches on the upper windows and he had gone the length of finding a ladder and leaving it in readiness. It did not reach the windowsills, but there was a nest of drainpipes which he used as footholds. Seconds later he was levering up one of the bedroom windows.

'Resourceful chap, that.' Staring up angrily at the dark lithe figure now swinging itself under and in, I had forgotten that I was not alone. My companion seemed to think this an exploit, to me it was quite the reverse.

'I don't think I want to,' I said when the hall door opened and Martin bade us enter.

He glanced at me shrewdly. 'Please yourself. But don't leave the door open.'

Again I lacked the courage of my convictions. Martin ushered his friend along the creaking floorboards of the hall and into the drawing-room, and I went after them. It was years since I had been in the house. Hew had showed me round it once, but he had not been able to answer any of my eager questions about the family, and I had wondered afterwards if my curiosity had perhaps been the cause of my never being taken there again.

Today it had a musty feel which repelled me. And then I looked up at the wall above the fireplace and everything else went out of my head.

The girl in the painting hung over the room like a bird poised for prey. That was the genius of it. Wonderful and terrifying.

Wonderful because the tawny gold waist-length hair and the long wide sleeves falling back from the upraised arm moved as I looked at them, or I could have sworn they did. Terrifying because the hand was holding a sword, glinting and quivering and about to crash down on us.

I blinked and came to myself to find somewhat unnervingly that my two companions were gazing not at the picture but at me.

'Is that Hew's?' I gasped.

'Don't you know?' Martin retaliated.

Why was he looking at me so intently?

'No, I don't know. I've never seen it before,' I answered.

'But surely . . .' Now it was the turn of the art expert. 'My dear young lady, surely you were the model?'

'Me?' It was ludicrous. 'Of course not. I don't look like that.'

The girl in the picture, as I stared defiantly up at her, was for one thing a different shape. Where I was slender, verging on boyishness, she was full-breasted, even a trifle 'hippy'. The loose blue green gown showed every line. Apart from that, there were the eyes. Mine are quite ordinary, hers – well, I couldn't describe them. They were like a cresting sea, half green, half blue. No words really got what Hew had put into them – light, darkness and storm and somehow the feeling that they were braking the arm.

As long as those eyes saw what they did, the sword might tremble but would not fall. All *I* could see for my pains was the corner of something like a couch and on the floor beside it a helmet.

'It's a very exciting picture,' I said lamely.

'It's a very exciting girl,' Martin appended, chuckling.

He conducted the owner of the gallery back to his car. I guessed they wanted to talk and, in a strange way, my priorities of making sure this was not some dirty business which would harm Hew had transferred themselves to the girl who was looking down at me. I felt bound up in her.

She was not myself; I had not suffered the storms her face reflected. It was paradoxically a very young face, rounder and more childish than mine, yet fully adult. Irrational as it might seem, I was shaken. I knew that to me in future she would stand for the spirit of Haresmead, a troubled, violent spirit, conflicting utterly with my cosy romantic dreams.

The thing that shook me even more was the suggestion that there was a personal connection between us.

'You recognize her, of course?' Martin's voice behind me made me jump. 'Isolde.' He came over and stood at my side.

21

'Isolde?' I echoed. All I could think of was an opera. I did not even know the music. Just two names — Tristan and Isolde.

'You should know,' Martin reproved. 'She was Irish, the daughter of a king. One day she gave shelter to a stranger, a wounded knight called Tristan, not knowing that he had received his wounds in combat with her lover whom he had slain. When the discovery came to her, her first thought was to kill Tristan with his own sword while he lay helpless on the couch.' He paused and involuntarily we both looked up.

'And did she?' I asked.

'No, that would have left Wagner two acts short for his opera,' Martin returned lightly. 'Tristan opened his eyes at the crucial moment and as she looked at him hatred fused into . . .'

'Love?' I was surprised to find myself supplying the word.

'Not so fast. That comes in the second act,' he said smoothly. 'Shall we say "desire"?'

It was infuriating to find that I had blushed. 'I wonder whatever made Hew paint her,' I said to change the subject.

'I wonder why he didn't show us Tristan,' Martin responded dryly.

Unexpectedly after he had closed the door of Haresmead behind us he walked part of the way home with me.

'Keep this to yourself,' he commanded abruptly as we left the woods and came out on the hill behind the graveyard. 'All of it.'

'That depends,' I retorted rashly. 'I won't stand by and see Hew cheated. If you're planning . . .'

'Planning?' Surprise, either real or cleverly feigned, gave dark eyes and cheekbones an angled look. 'What, pray? An art swindle? I'm afraid you flatter him. My sole purpose in coming here was to winkle him out.'

'I thought so!' I exploded angrily. 'May I ask what divine right you have to interfere?'

'None.' He blew on his hands, thrusting them into the pockets of his black leather coat. 'But I'm effective.'

'How effective?'

He considered me. 'You'll find out – when the time comes. It won't for a while.'

I was staring at him mute with anger and disturbed when we heard the sound of a horn and minutes later the hunt streamed into view. Hounds swept the covert just below us, someone shouted: 'Tally-ho!' and we saw a fox streaking out across country. I spotted the Master whom I knew well amongst the pink coats and my father in the middle of a bunch of black ones. It was pretty evident that particular fox would get away.

'Pleased?' Martin asked mischievously. It recalled his intuitive glance on the night of our party.

To break my rule would have been treason. I certainly wouldn't do so for the likes of him. 'You must keep things in proportion,' I said defensively. 'Better a fox than one of the hounds, better a hound than a horse.'

'I see. Ascending scale. What if it's a man?'

'It never is, thank goodness,' I answered carelessly.

A patronizing twinkle crept into his eyes: 'I do believe beneath that manly bosom there lurks a woman's heart.'

'Well, I don't know what else it could be,' I said crossly. He had a wretched way of making me feel just a kid and even of making me wish my old red anorak changed into sleek dark leather with a fur lining. 'Oh, I was supposed to ask you and Hew to supper,' I remembered ungraciously. 'Tomorrow, if that suits.'

Martin was sure it would suit Hew. 'Unfortunately I already have a date. But please thank your mother; I'll see her before I go.'

Mummy and he, I had to admit, had clicked at first sight.

It didn't worry me that he wouldn't be coming. Jolly good luck to the girl, whoever she was, she'd need it. But that was it, *who was she?* Where had he met her? Where were they going? Was she someone I knew?

'Eileen Connaughton,' Hew told us at supper the following night. 'I didn't even know they knew each other, but that sort of thing never takes Martin long!'

The Connaughtons were farmers and good ones. Eileen was a few years older than me, miles more attractive and a big success with the boys.

'Like calls to like, eh?' my father grinned.

'Just so,' Hew agreed.

It was fair comment. Martin's surface assets were considerable – that car and those Sacha Distel looks. As I
thought of it, Mummy said: 'You know it's not fair.
Martin's *too* dishy. He shouldn't have free range!'

'Handsome is as handsome does,' I clipped in darkly.

'Oh, he does very handsomely too,' Hew remarked.
'He'll retire at thirty-five – if he lives that long.' He added
that Martin's longer than usual Christmas break this year
was on doctor's advice. He needed to unwind.

Mummy inquired in a carefully casual tone about
Martin's family.

'Only child,' Hew told her. 'His parents are alive and
well and living in America. Not together, I would add.'
He turned the conversation by asking Dad if he was going
out with the staghounds next day. Martin had taken a
visitor's cap, largely, I gathered, on the persuasions of
Eileen Connaughton.

My father said he would have to miss the meet. He had
been out yesterday and could not spare the time so soon
again.

'Judy?' Hew invited. 'Martin is lending me the
yoke.'

I accepted with alacrity. Never before had I had the
chance of following the hunt in such style. Drive up in
Martin's billowing silver 'yoke' and we would be the envy
of all.

When day dawned there was nothing to prepare me for
the horrendous memory it would become. The weather-
men's prophecy of a spell of quiet weather had been
fulfilled. The fields were a cold wet green and the air was
utterly still. Fishbone branches webbed a pallid sky. I remembered learning a poem once about 'Meath of the pas-
tures'.

The meet was at twelve-thirty, outside the Stag's Head,
and when Hew and I arrived heads turned in astonishment and several people asked if he had won the pools.

I suppose it's because I have always had an in-
volvement with an artist's brush that scenes like that one

paint themselves on my mind. There was the forecourt with the old sign above the pub, Johnny the landlord bringing out his tray of drinks, hounds weaving round the horses' legs and everyone's breath curling out in front of them on the cold air. I had a personal fondness for the staghounds. The Master and the officials kept up the tradition of black silk hats with their scarlet coats, and it added something to the occasion.

Today they were out after an outlier stag which had escaped them last time and had been living wild for a month. There would be no kill because stags were not expendable, and indeed I had often seen hounds fawn on the stag they had cornered.

Martin and Eileen Connaughton had ridden up together and were in a group not far away from where Hew had parked. Prince's coat shone like copper. I had never seen him in better fettle. He was a game little pony, good-tempered and brave. I always thought of him as mine, which was, of course, ridiculous.

After a bit Eileen walked her big grey over to the car. We knew each other slightly and we chatted.

'I've been telling Martin he must come back at Easter,' she confided. 'You'll second that, won't you, Judy?'

'It's nothing to do with me,' I said flatly.

'I know, but make him feel he's wanted,' she chided.

Somehow I couldn't answer. A power outside myself clamped down on the polite lie. Martin was a disturber of the peace. I did not want him to come back, and he knew it.

From Prince's back he gave me a long slow look. The black cap sat easily on his crisp dark hair, its chin-strap emphasizing the colour in his face. It was midwinter, but he looked as though he had been lying out in the sun. A pale blue tinge to his shirt flattered the brown of his neck.

'Let me reassure you,' he said amusedly. 'We may never meet again.'

'I'm sorry, I didn't mean to be rude.' It was to Hew I made my belated apology.

'Don't worry,' he soothed. 'He's used to it. In his world you don't expect to be liked.'

I considered what a far cry that world was from Dunbeagle where even in these days we all had a lot of time for each other. 'Could you stand that?'

'Me? I wouldn't last a week,' Hew laughed.

'Nor me. In fact, I've been thinking I could always stay here and help Dad.'

'I'd say he wouldn't let you.' Hew looked over his shoulder as the hunt began to move off. 'You must go away, Judy. I believe you have a fine future. You won't find it here.'

'You make me sound like *him*.' I glanced resentfully at Martin's smooth black back.

'Perhaps you are,' Hew said strangely. 'You both fight enough, if that's anything to go on.'

'Sometimes you have to,' I defended myself.

'I don't,' he pointed out. 'It's tiring.'

Quite true, I owned, as we drove off in the wake of the company. You couldn't fight with Hew if you tried. How often had we urged him to stand up for himself with the owners of Haresmead and get a bath installed.

'Anyway, don't *you* ever go away,' I concluded. 'Because wherever *I* go I shall come back. I know I shall.'

'Please the pigs,' he appended solemnly. 'Your Ancient Monument will be waiting!'

It sounded sad, and candidly, these holidays Hew had looked his age. His face was actually more lined than my father's, though he was ten years younger. 'Martin is appalled at the way Hew lives,' Mummy had said a few days ago. 'He says he has no idea how to look after himself.'

It was worrying, but since hounds had now left the road and were streaming across country the hunt was really on and keeping up with it demanded all my skill as navigator.

It was a long smooth chase. The escapee stag was sighted after half an hour and for the next two managed to elude capture. It was after four o'clock, and growing dusk, when we approached a village. The hunt skirted it, wheeling out to the right. Hew accelerated and we tore down the main street. Had we lost them? No. We were in luck.

Where the main body of the hunt was behind us making their last circling manoeuvre, the stag was along-

26

side us in a field on our right. For all the hours that had passed he was still fresh and running strongly. A few breakaways from the hunt were galloping down the grass verge, among them Martin and Eileen.

Eileen's big grey was noted for his going and she pushed every able inch of him. She was a marvellous rider. I wasn't, much as I loved tagging along, and I had never got as much out of Prince as Martin was getting at this moment. The little chestnut was going like greased lightning. It was a revelation. Prince travelling like that! First I felt incredulous, then outraged.

The stag had been flying along, leaping the sheep wire and outdistancing his pursuers. Suddenly he turned left and jumped out on to the pavement. Hew braked and the horses on the grass verge thundered past. The stag checked the road and crossed. The wall of the churchyard ran along on the left. He cleared it with ease. The horses were only seconds behind him. I caught my breath as first Eileen's horse and then Prince soared over the wall.

Hew said nothing, but his face changed. He ran the car to the lych gate and we tumbled out. To make matters worse there was a funeral in progress. All but the priest and the chief mourners had run. Startled faces stared down the rows of gravestones. The stag had run to the back wall and leaped it. The two horses were still clattering perilously between the headstones.

'There's a ditch!' I shouted. *'Mind the ditch!'*

I couldn't have stopped myself, but it was useless except as a death knell. As the words left my lips Eileen drove the grey at the wall and Martin followed. I saw him rise in the saddle and the lovely cream flash of Prince's tail. As they disappeared I heard Eileen scream.

'Judy, no!' Hew caught my arm. 'Stay here.' He pinioned me. I shook him off and ran.

Not Prince, not Prince, I sobbed under my breath.

It was full dusk in the field behind the church and the hunt had ended. The hounds, trained not to kill, had cornered their quarry. Grasped by the back legs, it was being shuffled into the trailer box to be returned to the deer park and another day.

Martin was being helped away, his left hand was hanging and I had seen blood on his face, but he had had a miraculous escape. 'Must have nine lives,' someone said in my hearing.

Prince had had only one life, and it was over. He had broken his neck.

Grief stunned me.

'I'll get you another horse,' Hew comforted. 'A better one. It will be all right, honey, I promise you. We'll look for it straightaway. The best won't be good enough, Judy. We'll find you a champion.' I felt his arms go round me, but none of it meant anything because I was still in a daze.

'I don't want it. Don't be silly,' I said roughly.

My parents blamed Eileen – she was familiar with the terrain and should have known better. Those who had seen the accident said Martin had ridden brilliantly, putting himself at risk to avoid the funeral party. I suppose I accepted the facts, but none of them eased the pain. I hated Martin Trelawney as I had never hated anyone in my life.

He had to go to hospital to have his wrist set, but they discharged him on Sunday morning and Hew called on the way home to reassure Mummy that all was well. I saw her go out to the car, but couldn't bring myself to follow. She came back disturbed because Martin looked shaken and there was no comfort in 'that place of Hew's'. 'I wanted him to come here, but he wouldn't. I wonder if the Connaughtons have asked him?'

'How was Hew?' I asked. I was not particularly proud of those rough few minutes when I had pushed away his arms and spurned his comfort, but inexplicably the kindness had made it worse. For me Prince could never be replaced. I had cried like a baby all night.

However, it was an agony for which I must not punish Hew and I wanted to say my piece before I had to set off in the morning for England and school.

As I took the old bridle path over the hill to Haresmead a car went down the lower road and I recognized Eileen Connaughton as the driver. Though I could not be absolutely certain I thought her passenger was Martin.

28

When I got to the cottage the key was in the door. I turned it and went inside. It was not completely dark, but at home Mummy had a thing about half light, it gave her the creeps. I had left behind me a warm bright room.

Hew had no lights on, the fire in the kitchen was low and only silence greeted me. It seemed a very sad, very empty place. At least I thought it was empty until I pressed the light switch.

Hew had an old couch against the wall. Martin was stretched out on it – asleep. He looked pale and his wrist was plastered and in a dark silk sling, but he was alive. Prince, dear spunky Prince, was dead.

To this day I can remember how I stood there, filled with bitterness, my hatred seething on the surface. Why couldn't he have been killed instead of Prince?

Two of the model soldiers were on the chimneypiece, 'Darius' in his spotted blue tunic and the proud Prussian on his dark brown horse. They were about the only things I had seen Martin care about.

He deserved, I thought, to be made to suffer. He deserved to know the ache I was feeling for someone I had loved. It would be only a little pain compared with Prince, but he should have it.

I took the Prussian off the mantelshelf and held him above my head. The bigger the fall the better. The weight of the casting would gather impetus. The delicate eagle wings, the helmeted head, the horse's legs and the pennon-crowned lance would smash into smithereens.

But could I destroy them? I loved craftmanship, and this was nearer to a work of art. A piquant revenge it might be, but the scales were weighted against me. I could never demolish a thing so precise and perfect. Slowly I dropped my arm.

Martin's eyes had opened. He could have shouted, he could have grabbed my arm. But he did nothing.

I cannot put the moment into words. It is enough to say that, hate him as I did, I couldn't find one of the words that had stayed all night on my tongue. He actually seemed to have changed so that I saw how slender he was under the belt, how a blunt nose made his face less severe and how his dark eyes seemed to arch under their smooth brows.

Two minutes ago I had wished him dead, now he mesmerized me.

I hate him, I thought, and my eyes fell. I was bewildered, ashamed and trembling. 'The fire's gone down,' I said lamely, and picked up the coal bucket.

'Thank you.' There was no need for him to say more. I knew he understood perfectly what I had been about to do. I could only pray he had missed the mixed-up crazy emotion which had overtaken me.

I placed the last lump of coal and straightened.

'You were right.' The voice was so quiet I hardly recognized it. 'As you said, it never is the man. Doubtless you would now add: Worse luck.'

'That would be wrong,' I said shortly.

To my astonishment he reached out with his uninjured arm and clasped my wrist. 'I'm terribly sorry,' he said.

I nodded. I knew he was, though minutes ago I would have scorned any such saving grace.

'It was quick. He knew nothing,' he added.

'I know,' I said softly. That last flash of tail as Prince had soared, as you might say, into oblivion, would stay with me for ever. Now it was my undoing. The tears welled into my eyes. Damn! It was the last thing I wanted him to see.

Intuitively he made no comment, but his hand slipped into mine and linked my fingers. 'It won't always hurt like this.' The grip said more than the words.

My own words were as sparing and difficult to say. 'At least – he was enjoying himself. I never saw him go like that before.'

Something flickered through Martin's eyes. 'That's generous.' He looked round a little vaguely. 'Now what about some tea? I can manage, given a bit of time.'

'Nothing for me, thanks,' I said breathlessly. 'I'm expected home. It's my last day.' It was part of the confusion that the olive branch was more disturbing than the acrimony.

'As you wish,' Martin responded equably. 'It's goodbye, then, and good luck.' He hesitated, his hand still holding mine. 'Take this as it's meant, Judy. You're not short on warmheartedness, match it with common sense. Get away from here and you'll go far.'

'Thanks,' I said awkwardly, slipping my hand away. 'I'll – work it out. Good-bye!'

At the door something made me turn round. He was looking straight at me and he smiled.

'Good-bye – Isolde!' he said.

CHAPTER TWO

THE bus always gave a sickening lurch on the bend into the village. As it did so now, my head jerked and all my ghosts were gone. Two of them, I thought happily, would soon be replaced by the real thing. Directly I had seen Dad I would make for Hew's cottage. A bittersweet homecoming it might be, but at that moment joy pushed sorrow away.

The two people closest to me were now so near.

There was a big tree on the grass near the Stag's Head. I was so cock-a-hoop with excitement that I almost looked to see if they had tied a yellow ribbon round it to tell me I was welcome. It has always been a favourite of mine, that song, and it rang in my head as I started gathering my things together.

> 'The whole dam' bus is cheering and I can't believe I see
> A hundred yellow ribbons round the old oak tree.'

Of course if you *will* come home like a thief in the night, I pointed out to myself as I shouldered the kangaroo. There were no yellow ribbons but, praise heaven, there was Dunbeagle, the Stag's Head, the granite spire of the church and the road home.

The first sight of our house gave me a stab. I knew it had been repainted – Mummy had written about the colour scheme a month before she died – but I'd forgotten. The new sealing wax red on the door was very smart but, oh dear, she should have been there to hear me say so. Never mind. In two shakes Dad would be goggling at me and then flinging out his arms and crushing me against his chest. It was the thing I remembered most about coming home for the holidays, Dad standing still with his arms out and myself rushing into them.

His car was not in the drive and the open gates gave me my first cold shiver. It was to be expected that he might be out on a call or up at the golf club where I knew he spent a lot of his spare time, but I hadn't really bargained for it.

I thought: *'If I don't see a yellow ribbon round the old oak tree, I'll stay on the bus . . .'*

What nonsense! I had a latchkey. If nothing else the *contretemps* justified the sentimental foible that had made me keep it. I used it now and went in. The first step into the hall was enough to tell me that the house was full of emptiness. A few more steps and what had seemed a temporary setback acquired scaring significance.

It was all so tidy, everything in its place, no sign of Dad's pet trademarks, pipe or laid-down newspaper. In the back of the house the curtains were half drawn, obviously to keep the sun off the dining-room carpet. Dad wouldn't have thought of that in a million years! And in the kitchen all the pans were neatly racked and the sink rubber was hanging up bone dry.

As it hit me, I pulled up a chair and sat down. The house had been cleaned through and no human hand had sullied it. My father was away.

I couldn't hardly complain about it. I had so persistently urged him to take a holiday. In fact, once I had discovered where he was, it might be feasible to follow him. He would have left an address in case of emergency. Our home help in the past had been Mrs. O'Driscoll from the cottages. I could call on her if Hew didn't know.

Hew came first.

He was like the latchkey, I thought as I sponged my travel stains. Say 'Dunbeagle', and, snap, I saw Haremead and the little damp cottage where I had no doubt the cold tap still needed a washer.

I was too tired to change out of the trousers and the shirt jacket I'd travelled in and lately I'd lost a bit of weight. In short, what I saw in the mirror was not exactly Miss World. The only good thing about this crazy home-coming was the fact that the bed in my old room was made up. It looked almost as though Dad had had a hunch that I might walk in.

I thought about making a cup of tea, decided against it and went out. A few minutes of fast walking took to 'my' view. The green hill above the churchyard, the coloured hills of Caoindruim scalloping the skyline, and the blue dome of sky. Meath has the best cattle land in Ireland, so my hill was the very heart of green.

It was a view that always seemed to be flying, especially when the wind whistled the gorse or a jet cut a foam track on the blue.

This evening my mind saw it before my eyes did. A second later I stopped, incredulous. There was a sign board half-way up the hill. It read:

ICEBERG (IRELAND) LTD.
A member of the Iceberg Group.

What a daft place, I thought, to put a sign. Whatever Iceberg (Ireland) might be, it was not there, so why stick up a notice about it in the middle of nowhere? And why had Hew allowed it? It was an eyesore. Oh, heavens, I thought, troubled, don't say they're getting rent for it! His cheeseparing employees were so indifferent to Hares-mead that they could well have agreed to the wretched board being erected.

I walked on quickly, feeling cross.

The path, as always, dived into the woods, but it took only a matter of yards to sense uneasily that something was different. For one thing, no birds were twittering though always at this hour the trees would be full of them settling down to roost. And for another thing, the trees themselves were surely not as dense as they used to be.

A cold hand touched my heart and receded. My cheeks burning, I broke into a run.

I don't think I shall ever forget the moment when I burst into the clearing.

Hew's cottage was gone. It had apparently vanished without trace.

You know the way you look at a thing and think you are dreaming. I did just that, and then inexorably the truth dawned. I saw the felled trees, the wheel tracks, the clodded earth and the bulldozer. And when I ran on to the big house there was another board with the same legend.

ICEBERG (IRELAND) LTD.
Opening March 1976.

I hammered on the front door, but there was no reply. I had not expected one. Hew was gone, and never had I needed him so much.

Happily Dunbeagle had no lack of kindness. Down at the cottages Mrs. O'Driscoll opened the door and beamed. 'Yes, that's why I washed the curtains,' she said when I inquired if Dad were away. 'I don't know where you call it,' she added when I asked where. 'I think someone asked him.'

She handed me a slip of paper and I read it with a feeling of disappointment.

'C/O Chards, St. Keir, near Wadebridge, North Cornwall,' my father had written. If Chards was the name of a house to which 'someone had asked him' it put paid to my impulsive thoughts of joining him there.

The news of Hew was equally daunting: 'Oh, he's gone. Someone told me they're building a big place up there.' She looked at me flatly. 'There's no food beyond in the house. The doctor told me to take what was left. I'd better go down to Burkes and give them a shout.'

Burkes, once the small village shop, had blossomed into a supermarket. Mrs. O'Driscoll went purposefully to the side door to knock up the owner and while I was waiting Father Connolly drove up, spotted me and stopped. Protests were futile. Before I knew it, I was sitting down to supper in the presbytery.

I had known the parish priest and his housekeeper for years. They were able to confirm that Dad was staying with a friend in Cornwall, and a further frustration was the news that he had left Dunbeagle only two days ago and was not due home for a fortnight. 'Don't mind that, though. He'll be back the moment he hears from you, that's for sure.'

I wondered how fair it would be. It had always been difficult to prise Dad away from his work. This year of all years he needed the rest and change.

'What are they doing to Haresmead?' I broke in. Father Connolly was not young. He had ministered a long time in Dunbeagle and I knew he loved it. Undoubtedly he would share my outrage at the despoliation.

Surprisingly he seemed to be of two minds. 'I know it's a pity to see it go, but old codgers like myself mustn't be selfish. People are getting it hard every way, whether they work the land or go up to Dublin, and anything within reason that's going to give employment is not to be sneezed at.'

Within reason? I echoed in silent rebellion.

'Anyway, what is Iceberg? I've never heard of it.'

'Sure, neither had I,' he admitted, twinkling. 'And I suppose I'd better get it right now, hadn't I? Delph, we used to call it when I was a boy. Nowadays it's ceramics.'

I was still too resentful to respond.

'You're shocked. I know. So was I at first,' he went on. 'And then I thought to myself it could have been pigs or glue.'

'What about Hew, Father?' I asked desperately. 'Do you know where he's gone?'

'He didn't write to you, then?'

'Not about this.' Except for a predictably warm and understanding letter at the time of Mummy's death I hadn't heard from Hew for more than a year, certainly not since I'd decided to go to Australia.

'No?' Father Connolly looked thoughtful. 'Well, I'm afraid I can't help you either. He said something to me one day about feeling like the prodigal son, but that's all I know. I never heard where he came from originally, but I took it he meant he was going back there. The doctor will know, though, you can depend on it.' He looked at me keenly. 'It's been no sort of homecoming for you, Judy, I realize that. But I don't think we need worry too much about Haresmead. I know it's a shame in ways, but they'll do a good job on the building. I was talking to the young fellow in charge the other day and he assured me it's had a lot of thought, and the County Council are well pleased with the plans.'

'I thought you'd be on my side,' I said reproachfully. Springs ago, even before Hew had come, Father Connolly had taken me up to Haresmead to spot the returning gold-crests.

'Always,' he rejoined, twinkling. 'So long as you don't let on to the Bishop!'

The telephone pealed and he went to answer it, coming back with a grin on his face. 'It's for you, Judy. The Other Channel!'

The Church of Ireland rector and his wife I had never met because they were only a year in the parish, but Mummy had been very fond of them and their baby daughter. Now word of my homecoming had reached them and they were inviting me to leave my empty house and stay at the Rectory. The rector wouldn't take no for an answer and put me on to his wife, who was equally pressing and only accepted my refusal with the proviso that I would ring at any time if I changed my mind. 'We feel we know you,' she ended. 'We knew your mother so well and she was so good to us when we were settling in.'

Here was someone, I thought, who could surely tell me about Hew. Alas, no. She knew only as much as everyone else, but she didn't stop there. She went on – and disquietingly.

'Wherever he is let's hope he's happier. I never saw such a miserable man.'

'Hew miserable? Never!' I gasped.

'Yes, well, of course I never got to know him. Not properly. It wasn't from want of trying, but he always seemed to shut us out. Your mother knew that. She was very concerned about him. Only latterly, I take it. She did say he'd changed a lot in the past year, and I know she wondered if there was anything she could do.'

'Oh, he must have known about Haresmead,' I interrupted distressfully. 'He must have known before it was made public. That's the answer. It would have broken his heart.'

'Hm. You could be right, I suppose, but he was like that when we came here, and that's a year ago.' She re-extended her invitation to me and rang off.

Father Connolly drove me home, my supermarket bag quite a bit heavier for the additions his housekeeper had made to it from the presbytery larder. The sun which that morning I had seen rise over the eastern Mediterranean slipped out of sight behind Caoindruim and I was alone.

In a mixed-up way I was too tired to think and too tired to stop myself. As I made the cocoa Father Connolly's housekeeper had recommended all my thoughts were in a tangled ball. I sat on the edge of the bed sipping my drink and trying to decide about getting in touch with Dad.

It was a trifling thing that set me off at last, the pink kangaroo that I had won in a raffle and had always seen myself bringing back to Mummy. She had had a passion for soft toys and would have adored it, especially the eyelashes. Now I looked at it on the bed and wondered what had possessed me to trail it home.

As I sat there in the empty house, my loss was final as it had never been.

I pushed away the beaker, got into bed and howled.

Mummy was only the first grief; I had a skein of sorrow at which my mind plucked weakly and ineffectually. I have always been one to cry for the underdog. And, let's face it, to expose myself wholeheartedly to risk.

I once made a pet of a young cockerel whose owner was keeping it for the pot. Believe it or not, I remembered it at that moment. I saw Prince lying in the ditch. And I saw Hew with his large rueful mouth and limp wind-blown hair. Hew, a friend to everybody, and so shamefully used.

I had cried very little when the news about Mummy had come. I cried now in a wet crazy hotchpotch, for her

37

and the kangaroo, for the cock and for Prince, for ruined Haresmead and for Hew. One began where the other left off.

The trouble was that once started I was quite unable to stop.

It must have made me a little mussy. I did think at one moment that I heard a car, but why not? I asked myself, the house was near the road and my window was open. Anyway, it didn't matter. Every nerve storm has a flash-point at which one lets go, and I was perilously near mine.

There were sounds, of course there were, the sleepy cackle of a bird awake for some reason, a car door slamming, a cat knocking something over. Cats were always jumping into the yard; in the past I had often mistaken their clatter for the banging of the hall door. But in the next second I felt the small hairs rise on my spine. I heard nothing. It just seemed to come to me through the wall that someone or something was creeping along the corridor.

I *had* heard a car, I *had* heard the hall door, *and* . . .

The door whipped open, the light flashed on, a man's voice said grimly:

'All right, I heard you. What's the game?'

I shot up like a jack-in-the-box. The man swung round. My jaw dropped, his eyes flew open. The hair was straighter than I remembered, but the dark eyes with their high pupils stood out as clearly as ever.

'Suppose you tell me, Martin Trelawney,' I suggested coldly.

He let the challenge go. 'Have you just arrived? From Sydney? Today?'

I nodded and he shook his head as though words failed him.

It made me feel very foolish. It also gave me feelings such as I had not had for weeks. Sandalwood, red wine and sunset. I have a mad brain, that's what it conjured up. That and a golden label reading something like this. 'Haughty Man. Produce of Jerez de la Frontera, Spain', and on it a face with sharp eyes and a clipped wing of hair. The black and white spotted tie and the black and white striped shirt which the original was wearing I tried not to see. They were defiantly London, England.

It is a known fact that Nasties make the best pictures. I was feeling better already until I remembered the face that I personally was behind. At that moment it was shiny and my eyes were all gummed up. Oh, heavens, what must I look like? It was monstrously unfair.

'And you?' I inquired belatedly.

'In from the mainland,' he said impishly. 'With my eye on that bed, as a matter of fact. Did your father not tell you I'd been keeping it warm for you?'

'My father is away.'

'I know. I have his permission to be here and a latch-key.' He held it up. 'The trouble is we didn't know about you. That's why I thought you were a burglar.' His gaze narrowed and to my further discomfiture he sat down on the bed. 'Look, why don't I fix you a drink? You look as though you could use one. And then I'll be off.'

'It's very late. If you want to stay the night, do,' I said, shrugging. 'I can put sheets on Dad's bed.'

'You wouldn't mind?' He looked surprised.

'I wasn't anticipating having cause to mind,' I answered tartly. 'If I thought I would have I'd lock the door. Anyway, please yourself. It will soon be morning.'

'And by the looks of you, you haven't had much sleep.' For the moment the voice could almost have belonged to Hew. 'I'll make that drink. Shall I bring it up?'

'No. I'll come down,' I said quickly. 'I want to talk to you.'

'Right.' He gave my leg a pat through the bedclothes and stood up. 'Toss you for the kangaroo. I've never slept with one.'

Damn! The silly thing was on the eiderdown. I'd forgotten about it.

'Oh, that was for Mummy,' I said without thinking.

Martin halted, the amusement leaving his face. 'That was a shame. I can't tell you how sorry I was when I heard. She had such a gift of gladness.'

'Thank you,' I said, astonished, as he closed the door.

In the minutes that were left to me I leaped out of bed,

washed my face and brushed my hair. There was no time to put it up, I swept back the top piece and clasped it, iced colour on my lips and slipped into a housecoat. Its colour, kingfisher blue, most green-eyed people can wear successfully. The combination of long greeny blue robe and long severe blonde hair made me think: 'Gracious, I am a bit like Hew's picture. I hope he packed it well, wherever he took it,' and then I ran downstairs.

'My word, that's a change for the better,' Martin remarked. 'Come back, girl of my dreams.'

'Hard luck,' I told him promptly. 'Did no one tell you? Eileen Connaughton got married to a farmer in Tipperary.'

'Eileen Connaughton?' he echoed scornfully. 'She was never in the running. I'm referring to the Isolde touch.'

I laughed. 'It's a simple suggestible. Big blonde, right colour garment. Did you ever find out who was Hew's model?'

'You were, of course. We told you.'

'And I told you no. It wasn't my face. Certainly not my expression.'

'You don't understand, do you?' he asked softly. 'You never did.'

'So there'll never be a better place for an explanation,' I retorted.

'Place, maybe, but not time.' I could have sworn the dark eyes were giving a message. 'There's none left, Judy. The time is past.'

If it was a message I didn't understand it. Whose time? What time? A crazy few minutes more than seven years ago when hatred had seemed to fuse into that strange awareness of a man and his body? Agreed, that time was past, but need he have said it so warningly?

'Have you retired?' I asked abruptly.

He started. 'Retired?'

'Hew said you would when you were thirty-five.'

'If you want to know how old I am,' he said indifferently, 'why not ask? I'm thirty and still living out of suitcases. Now come and have that drink.'

There was something ritual-like about the brewing. The whiskey came from a silver flask. He blended it with

40

hot water, some of the honey which Father Connolly's housekeeper had slipped into my bag, and juice from a lemon which Mrs. O'Driscoll had not removed. I switched the fire on and flames-that-never-were writhed above the red coals. I left the curtains undrawn on the silver garden. In two and a half hours it would be light.

The hot punch was restoring. I sipped it slowly and gratefully. 'I'm sorry for making an ass of myself. I'm afraid I react badly when the world turns upside down.'

'The world will be right side up in two weeks,' Martin assured me. 'Probably sooner. Your father is bound to come home.'

'But I'm not bound to tell him. I've almost decided not to.'

He cast me an inquiring glance.

'I came home to reassure myself,' I said carefully. 'Not to hitch up to his apron strings or to tie him to mine.' The silence encouraged me to continue. My father was hale and hearty and his life a full one. Thank goodness everyone so far had confirmed that he was coping magnificently. I knew already Mrs. O'Driscoll's worth, and as regards the practice the new secretary whom as yet I had not met (though Mummy had mentioned her warmly in dispatches) was apparently a tower of strength. 'I haven't come home to stay,' I concluded. 'But when I do move it won't be as far as Australia. That's out now there's just the two of us.'

'You're a wise young woman,' Martin pronounced. 'Even if you do take kangaroos to bed.'

'Now tell me about Hew.' I felt quite guilty at having talked so much about myself. 'Have you seen him? Where is he? Is he well?'

'Hew is a big subject,' Martin said evasively. 'Let's finish with you first.'

'We have finished,' I corrected. 'And I want to know how he is.'

'He's extremely well. Pretend I'm he,' Martin commended astonishingly. 'And justify the four years you've spent whacking a typewriter.'

'I've kept myself,' I said briefly. 'And I've been places.'

I named them all, including those I'd visited on holidays. 'I've used my eyes and my ears as well as my fingers. I had to do it this way because I couldn't have lived off Dad. And I couldn't start painting out of nothing. I had to have something behind me, something that I'd experienced. Later, of course, I hope to concentrate on art, but I make no apology for getting there in my own time.' It was my favourite soapbox. I stopped defensively.

Martin was smooth. 'No one should apologise for common sense. You're preaching to the converted. Though I should need to see proof before I commission you. Are you any good?'

'As a matter of fact,' I said evenly, 'I'm very good.' I would never have made the boast to Hew or my parents, but there was something about Martin Trelawney that evoked this untypical response.

'Let's put you to the test,' he drawled lazily. 'If I asked you to choose a design for me what would it be?'

The echoing of my own thoughts was uncanny. 'A label for a brand of sherry. I'd put your face on it in a light gold wash. The border would be red and gold and burnt sienna. And the name of the sherry would be Summer Of A Haughty Man.'

I think it was probably the first time he had ever been taken aback, and I enjoyed his expression. The dark eyes had a swimmy look and the face lengthened.

'A Spanish sherry, I hope?' he murmured fastidiously. 'And, I should like to think, a rare wine, well matured?'

'Fully matured,' I agreed caustically. 'We can be certain of that.'

The whiskey had sharpened my wits. I had taken it as medicine and certainly it had done its work. I glowed pleasantly from head to toe and though I had no illusions about my companion he had as certainly banished my blues. I felt a different woman.

Now as I looked back at him I found him staring at me. Suddenly his eyes had lost their sharpness and become boyish. Once they had winked at me, I remembered, while their owner sang.

'I think we should make sure,' Martin suggested.

'Ah! But I detest sherry,' I said firmly.

'This is a rare brand,' he responded softly.

And indeed it was. No one had ever kissed me like that before. I began by thinking dispassionately: 'Maestro in action', but as I felt myself drawn closer there was almost a sense of homecoming. Tenderness and ardour were as skilfully blended as the potion I had just drunk.

'What a pity I'm not in the wine business,' Martin said as he released me.

'What is your business? Hew never told me.' It was appalling that I had allowed myself to be sidetracked so expertly from Hew, my first concern.

'Hew is my business,' Martin answered lightly. 'At least he is for the moment. I came a few weeks ago to rescue him.'

'You mean when they sold Haresmead over his head?'

There was a fractional hesitation. 'Eventually. I came first because your mother wrote to me. She didn't tell you?'

'I think – she can't have had time,' I said hardly.

'Yes, I expect so,' he agreed, watching my face. 'Well, that's all really. She was anxious and she got in touch. I came, and not a moment too soon.'

I could accept that. Hew would have been distracted. It was a safe bet he would have been too upset to care about eating or sleeping. And it was kind of Martin, busy as he was, to have answered Mummy's call. I said so and he brushed it aside looking embarrassed.

'So – where is Hew now?' I questioned.

'He's in St. Keir at present,' Martin replied airily. 'It's a village on the Camel estuary in the north of Cornwall.'

'But . . .' I had been trying to interrupt him, stuttering in excitement. 'But that's . . . *do you mean Dad and Hew are together?*'

'Yes,' he said innocently.

'But this changes everything.' Why couldn't he have said so at the beginning? 'I thought Dad was a guest in some house where I didn't know the people. If he's staying in Hew's house then of course I can go over.'

There was a suddenly strange silence. 'I suppose you

43

can,' Martin conceded with an obvious lack of enthusiasm. 'I nearly didn't tell you.'

'Why ever not?'

'Perhaps I wanted to keep you here, Isolde!' he suggested poker-faced.

'You can tell that to the marines, Tristan!' I flashed.

'Will *you* tell me something?' he retorted. 'Just for the record. Would you marry Hew?'

It was the second time within minutes that astonishment had winded me. It was a baffling question – something that if need ever arose I would have to think about carefully – and certainly an intensely private one.

'I have no plans to marry anyone,' I said briefly. 'I expect to be far too busy.'

'Great expectations apart, then?' he persisted.

I was angry. It was unwarranted interference. 'You don't really expect me to answer that?'

'No, but I find it an interesting study.' He looked at me shrewdly. 'Did you ever consider what a sensitive plant he is?'

'I know they don't come any better,' I said steadily. 'As you should know too. He's been special to me from the first day we met. If you like he's my Sir Gawain.'

I doubted if Martin, the go-getter, would recognize the quote. His lips, however, were already framing it. ' "A very parfait gentil knight." '

'Exactly. That's Hew,' I reiterated. 'The rock I steer by. He'll cut off his right hand before he hurt me, and I'd do the same for him. Does that answer?'

There was a long pause. I couldn't fathom why Martin's expression should look slightly compassionate. 'It answers,' he said at last. 'And personally I'm bushed. Got a long hard day tomorrow. You won't mind, I trust, if I now repair to your father's bed?'

CHAPTER THREE

WHEN I woke next morning the room was bright with sunshine and the house soundless. The events of the previous night recalled themselves and I sat up. I felt rested, and it was no wonder. The hands of the clock at the bedside stood at twenty minutes past ten.

I was up in two shakes. I had gone to bed happy with the prospect of Cornwall and the good sleep had topped me up even more. I took a bath and found clean clothes, sprigged underwear, a blue and green tee-shirt, flared green pants.

Downstairs the kitchen was as tidy as Mrs. O'Driscoll had left it, but someone had set the table with a check cloth and laid a place at it. There was a grapefruit, beautifully segmented, and, to my delight, a basket of croissants. The basket was ours, but I knew my purchases of yesterday had not included either rolls or fruit. These must be Martin's rations brought along for his own sustenance.

At the table sat the kangaroo with a napkin tied round its neck.

'Idiot!' I said cheerfully, putting the light under the coffee which again had been left in readiness.

It wasn't half bad to come down and find yourself catered for. Martin Trelawney had unsuspected qualities. I had no notion where he had gone, but he had left a note suggesting that we have dinner together. I was disposed to accept if only because there were still many questions I wanted to ask.

Admittedly some of them were borderline. I had no right to pry, but I would never have credited Hew with affairs to be settled up. I was sure he had walked out of Dunbeagle as lightly laden as he had walked into it. The horse Black Eagle might conceivably be awaiting sale, but that was all I could think of. It was odd, because Martin had mentioned that a long hard day lay ahead.

Ploys of my own took me to early afternoon. They included a call at the Rectory and another on Dad's secretary to thank her for the many *ex gratia* jobs she had done.

I was walking home when a car drew alongside and the driver asked for directions to Haresmead. They were easily given since we were at the main gate. He thanked me, but hesitated. 'You don't happen to know if Mr.

Trelawney is still there?'

'Oh, I'm sorry, he left some weeks ago,' I returned.

The inquirer's face dropped, but only for a second. 'Ah now, please, I'm not as late as that. The appointment was for twelve, but I got a puncture.' He smiled. 'Sorry for annoying you. I'll find out.'

Light was dawning. 'I'm afraid I got the signals crossed. You must mean Mr. Martin Trelawney.'

'Yes. I'm from the insurance company.' He took a card from his pocket book. 'It's about Iceberg.'

He must have thought me a complete nitwit. I stood staring at him, barely comprehending what he was saying.

'The new factory they're putting up. As I say, I had an appointment to meet the architect and go over the plans with him, but I don't suppose they've waited. My name will be mud.' He must have spotted my looks, for he broke off. 'Don't mind my asking, but have I said something I shouldn't?'

'I'm not keen on desecration,' I said shortly. 'Did you see the view as you drove in? Iceberg will put paid to that.'

'Oh, I see.' My companion looked understandably anxious not to become involved. 'It's a shame, I know, but it happens all over. Thanks a lot.' He waved at me and reversed to turn into the gates.

I have no idea how long I sat on the hill above the churchyard. Never had the view looked lovelier. Irish skies are notoriously fickle but can be breathtaking. Today's sky was such a strong hyacinth that it cast a web over the gorselands trapping the gold with blue. It was like watching at a deathbed.

Seven years ago Martin Trelawney had come into this Eden. Then he had destroyed a horse. It had not been enough. He had looked round him (I remembered the afternoon the two of us had stood on this very spot and he had made an oblique reference to the time not being ripe) and planned this future mischief. When it suited his plans he had acted, presumably by going to the owners behind Hew's back.

Was there no justice? I asked myself bitterly; how

could such plunder be legal?

Presently I saw that I was not alone. Martin, the insurance surveyor and a third man, presumably the architect, were pacing the land above me.

'This is just to give you an idea,' I heard Martin say. 'This phase hasn't reached the drawing board yet. It's planned for 1979.'

The last thing I wanted was to speak to him, and indeed, I did not expect to be noticed if I stayed exactly where I was and kept my back turned. Alas, a short time later I heard my name. Martin had left his companions and was coming down the hillside.

'Hallo there! Just to confirm the arrangement for tonight. I've booked for eight-thirty at the Abyssinian. I've eaten there with your parents, so I can vouch for it.'

'Did they know about this?' I blurted. It seemed impossible, and yet how could they not?

'If you mean my connection with Iceberg . . .' Martin was not slow-witted.

I did not let him finish. 'I mean this rape you're planning – that's what it amounts to – cold-blooded rape . . .'

'An inept comparison,' he said cuttingly. 'This concept in its initial stages will cost us half a million.'

'It will cost Dunbeagle its soul!' I retorted. 'And you haven't answered me. Did my parents know?'

'Please don't catechize me,' he said smoothly. 'Of course your father knows, your mother did too. Good grief, why should I keep it secret? It's a major event.'

'You kept it secret from me last night.'

'For the very good reason that you'd already had three shocks. Rest assured you'll hear all about it at dinner.'

'No,' I broke in. 'No, thank you. I'm not coming.' As he looked uncertain I spelled it out. 'Perhaps you don't realize I wouldn't be seen in public with you.'

Martin's face froze. 'In that case I'll cancel the table. The time will be useful. I need it.' He left me and went back to his colleagues.

In the wake of my brainstorm came swelling unrest. The house was speckless, so I went into the garden. Same story. Mrs. Burns, Dad's secretary, liked gardens and had

47

shown her liking in the nicest possible way. There was little to be done, but I pottered.

It was evening before my ears caught the sound they had been dreading – a car coming up the drive. I looked round the corner in time to see Martin get out and make for the hall door. He rang the bell and yielding to an absurd panic I raced back to the flowerbed I was weeding. I was too tired, I told myself, to face another row. Besides, he had a latchkey.

He had, and he must have used it. In minutes I heard the kitchen door being opened. Martin, grip in hand, came walking towards me.

I felt no pity for the dark town suit, neat cream shirt, tie and leather shoes on what had been the hottest day in Ireland so far that year.

'I'm off now,' he said.

'Off?' I echoed stupidly.

'To the Abyssinian. I'm staying there tonight. The invitation is still open if you care to change your mind.'

'No, thanks.' I did not want to look at him. Once before he had laid siege to my emotions by appearing vulnerable. Today the new cut to his hair gave him a semi-frown.

'You wouldn't work on the premise that we all need help rather than vendettas?'

'I wasn't thinking of a vendetta,' I said truthfully. 'And I don't wish to be discourteous, especially in this house. If I was offensive this afternoon I apologize. But that's not to say we're friends. It's just a truce contingent upon our not discussing Haresmead.'

'Were you afraid we might do that over dinner?'

'Dinner,' I said plainly, 'comes into the friendship zone.'

Martin made a moue. 'There appears, as always, the true word spoken in jest. Last night you called me Tristan!' He picked up the grip which he had laid down. 'Before I go I wonder if I might make a phone call?'

I said: 'Of course,' and thought no more about it. Shortly afterwards he called me. 'Someone to speak to you!' The receiver was off the hook.

I took it with a questioning: 'Hallo?'

'Tell me, cobber,' said the voice at the other end, 'is there a wild colonial girl your end, because I want to talk to her?'

It was my father.

The decision, it seemed, had been taken out of my hands. There was a plane next morning to Exeter. Martin would be travelling on it and had secured a seat for me. He had left his car in Exeter on the way over, we would pick it up and drive the rest of the way. Dad thought I was as mad as a hatter to have packed in Australia, but I could tell he was pleased, and Hew took the phone for a minute to say that the fatted calf was at that moment putting its affairs in order.

Not quite twenty-four hours and I would see them both. I knew Haresmead would continue to haunt me, but love and affection are the best medicine in the world.

'It was kind of you to arrange the flight,' I told Martin. 'But please let me go by train from Exeter. There's no reason why you should go to St. Keir.'

'Except one,' he responded. 'I live there.'

'Near Hew's house?' It was a dismaying thought.

'It's mine, actually,' Martin replied with the first diffidence I had ever seen in him. 'But it's always been in the family. It's as much Hew's, I assure you.'

'But not in fact.' For me facts had to be recognized. 'In fact Dad is *your* guest?'

'I have that pleasure.' I had a feeling he meant it. 'And despite all appearances to the contrary I value his having come. After tomorrow I hope to be able to stay home and entertain him. And you. Have you ever been to Cornwall?'

'No.'

'I'm glad,' he said disarmingly. 'You're in for a treat.'

It was an impossible situation. Last night's 'sweet talk' had been no more than a game. Today's full knowledge made it obnoxious.

'Take care, your charm is showing,' I warned him. 'And as to St. Keir, it would be out of the question for me to be a guest in your house. Either I stay at a hotel—'

'And have people conclude you don't get on with your

49

father,' he put in deftly.

I felt myself redden with irritation. 'Either I stay at a hotel or I pay my way.'

Martin burst out laughing. 'Don't be ridiculous!'

It might seem so, but there was a question of morals. I could not accept hospitality from a man I detested. It was different for Hew. He had been made homeless. I could even adjust to Dad being Martin's guest. He would not have put him up in Dunbeagle had he not considered the situation and come to terms with it.

But that was the crunch. Dad had never been involved with Haresmead as I had. I could not come to terms. I might not win, but I must stand up and be counted. 'It's a matter of principle,' I said.

'I can't take money from you,' Martin stated as flatly. 'You're reducing this to absurdity.'

The absurdity lay in thinking I could put myself under an obligation to him. I said this patiently and repeated it several times. It mattered very much.

'It still strikes me as hot air,' Martin said scathingly. 'But if you mean it – all right, there is something you could do.' He looked at me shrewdly. 'You won't like it, but it would more than compensate for your miserable bed and board.'

'Tell me.' I watched the gleam in his eye.

'Come to St. Keir as my fiancée.'

I blinked. I must be crazy, but I was sure I had heard him.

'Oh, don't get me wrong,' he went on silkily. 'The contract would be short-term, not life.'

'So that you could *use* me?'

His mouth twitched. 'Something like that.'

'I wonder you have the nerve!' I hurled furiously.

'Engage my feelings and you'll find my nerve is limitless.'

'It's a discovery I can dispense with,' I told him sharply. 'You must look elsewhere for your pawn. I don't play at love.'

'A pity,' he sighed. 'You did so well at the test. No don't slap my face, that's so stereotyped. And it is a pity. Now I'm serious. Clare is a fine person.'

'Clare?' I echoed.

'A friend of mine whose life has come to a crossroads.' He paused. 'Impetus is the word, I think.'

I could be sure it was. I was to be dandled in front of some female to make her see what she was missing. Who but Martin Trelawney would dream up such a ploy?

'Funny, I wouldn't have said marriage was your game,' I remarked acidly.

'Have I said it is?' he cornered coolly. 'However, you don't wish to take part, so that's an end to it. I'll pick you up in the morning about ten. Security checks take time these days.'

'But I'm not going,' I said hopelessly. 'Get that into your head. The conditions still stand.'

There was a long silence, or at least it seemed so, before he spoke again. Two words, curt and uncaring. 'Suit yourself.'

I thought the matter had ended, but as he turned to go he said in a blank tone,

'They'll be starting on the house next week. You were fond of it, I know. Is there something you'd like for a keepsake?'

I was astonished, first that he had made the offer, second that he had the power to dispose of the contents. Surely the owners of the property . . .

'Obviously you haven't seen the place lately,' Martin returned. 'There's nothing worth saving except the painting.'

'The Isolde?' I gasped. 'Are you offering me the Isolde? But that's Hew's.'

'He doesn't want it.' There was a pause. 'Do you?'

Did I? I was staggered at the thought of possessing such a lovely thing.

'I shall treasure it always.'

'It was a singularly unproductive phase,' Martin said carelessly. 'However, let's go.'

As we walked to the car, he plucked at the knot of his tie, pulled it loose and stuffed it into his pocket.

'Would you have liked a cup of tea?' I asked belatedly.

'About as much as you'd have liked to give it me,' he

answered shortly.

It was my first sight of Haresmead from its main approach. The undergrowth on the drive had been reduced, but not enough to dismay me, and the evening light was kind to the neglected lawns. It was no showpiece, but I loved it still.

'How did Hew react to the sale?' I asked hardly. 'I take it it was you who went to the owner?'

'Yes. I don't think he liked the idea to begin with, but I accept change resistance. I'm used to it. And now that he's got the chance to rebuild his life he's looking forward to it.'

There are none so blind as those who won't see or who choose to cast everyone in their own unfeeling mould. I knew it could not have been as easy as that, though even I could only guess at what Hew must have suffered.

The car rounded the bend in the drive and pulled up in front of the old house. It was deplorable. Slates were gone from the roof and one of the windows was broken. The railings each side of the steps were rusting away and the grass was growing merrily through the cracks in the stable yard. I could have cried for the degradation and decay.

'Who owned it?' I burst out impulsively. 'What kind of moron let it die like that?'

'You must allow that people can't afford to keep up big houses these days,' Martin said temperately. 'The outlay is considerable.'

'That's no excuse,' I flashed. 'It was sound when they got it, whoever they are. They just didn't care, did they? A few cans of paint would have saved those railings and it's not difficult to put in a pane of glass.'

'That's roughly what I thought seven years ago,' Martin commented.

I shot him a glance of suspicion. 'We're not getting at Hew. He couldn't have done anything. I know he was the caretaker, but he had no funds.'

'So you'd agree that the best thing has happened. Put it out of its misery?'

'Certainly not.' He was clever, but he wouldn't catch me that way. 'That's the biggest tragedy. All these years it has waited and now it's going to be bulldozed. It should be restored and given back to the village as a national park.'

'The weak point in that is that no one did it,' Martin pointed out equably. 'How many millionaires have you got in Dunbeagle? Pick your steps here. The stone is crumbling.'

It was another sad truth. The curving steps to the front door were also wearing away.

Martin turned the key and walked in on a creaking floorboard. The smell of must was overpowering. I followed, mindful of his injunctions to watch my step. It was like entering a tomb.

He opened the door of the drawing-room and I caught my breath. Copper sun rays were striking the fireplace wall and the Isolde painting seemed alive. I had forgotten how good it was. Today's vivid light showed powerful new undertones. Or was it that seven years had taught me not only more about painting but more about life?

'I can't believe Hew has left it behind,' I deprecated.

'See for yourself,' Martin gestured. 'He's left behind more than the Isolde painting, Judith,' he added quietly.

The painting was high up and heavy to lift. He brought a chair, tested its seat and stood on it. He was still short of his goal, but by dint of stretching his hands reached the frame. He took hold very carefully, his body taut, his neck braced and golden against the open cream collar. My silly mind threw me a picture of a sailor spread-eagled in the rigging.

Then the picture came down to me and I grasped its sides.

The next few seconds were a blur. I heard Martin ejaculate and saw him jump. The chair fell over, one of its legs in two bits. Martin had sprung away from me, he landed, took a further step and seemed to drop through the floor.

I think I said something idiotic like: 'Are you all right?'

When I got the Isolde down and propped against the wall I saw the full score. Only Martin's head, shoulders and arms were visible, the rest of him was hanging somewhere underneath the floor. The sunshine round the picture must have blinded him when he had jumped into the dark side of the room. He had not seen, as nor had I until that moment, that there was an opening in the floor.

'Careful,' he warned as I started forward. 'It's rotten. I'm all right. Easy does it.'

Thank heaven he had managed to break his fall. I held my breath as he hauled himself up and wriggled back to floor level. The opening had been made designedly – perhaps to serve as inspection pit for wiring – but it emphasized the perilous condition of the boards. At any moment those to which Martin was clinging might crumble into dust. Beneath them lay a six-foot corridor of empty space and if Martin had fallen all the way I could only guess that he would have crashed through the basement ceiling.

The thought made me close my eyes. 'Are *you* all right?' Martin asked edgily. 'Did you get the picture?'

He had crawled out of the hole and was kneeling on the floor at my feet. Cobwebs smeared his shirt and the black wing of hair. He had been a few sawdusty inches from death, but he was as cold as a rattlesnake. Except that his Adam's apple was working more noticeably than usual. His throat had a warm look, smooth, silky, brown. Somehow I couldn't take my eyes from it.

'Are you sure you haven't hurt yourself?' I asked.

'Just my pride,' he returned, getting up. 'That will never be the same again.'

CHAPTER FOUR

I HAD the phone number of the house in St. Keir and I planned to ring Dad with my explanation. He would be disappointed; so was I. It was all the worse when I woke on Friday morning to a beautiful morning.

'Get up and go,' the blackbirds whistled as I made breakfast. Instead, I sat on rather gloomily, choosing my words for Dad.

The door was shut and it was some minutes before I realized that the phone in the sitting-room was ringing. I ran in and answered it.

'Judy?' There was no levity this time about "wild colonial girls". My father had a professional voice and I recognized it. 'It's about Martin, I can't get on to the hospital. How serious are his injuries?'

I stuttered; Dad was patient. Earlier that morning Martin had rung Hew from our nearest hospital. My father had gathered that he had gone along there last night after a fall and they had kept him for X-ray. Consequently he would have to cancel his flight.

'What about you?' Dad inquired. 'Hew says he'll meet you at Bodmin.'

'No, don't expect me,' I said quickly. 'I'll wait for Martin.'

As I put the phone down I wondered what had possessed me. While it had not been the right time to tell him that I would not be going at all, the impression I had given had been completely contrary.

Immediately, there was the problem of Martin in hospital. He would not be there if he had not thought of giving me the Isolde. I was no Florence Nightingale, but could I walk away?

Dad's propensity for mislaying car keys was providential. The spare set for which in the past Mummy had always been responsible was now held by his secretary, Mrs. Burns. Because of this, I would be able to take the car out of the garage.

When I got there, the hospital ward was full and at first glance I could not see Martin.

'Up there, miss.' The patient nearest the door had been taking good stock of me. 'Last bed. I think he's having a doze.' As I hesitated he grinned. 'Go on, give him a shout. He'd never forgive you if you didn't.' It showed how thoughts ran if you were blonde with a large bun, a soupçon of fringe and a midi suit.

I went up the ward as directed. Martin's head was densely black against the starched pillow. He was lying on his back with his eyes closed and the sheet drawn over his chin. As I stood wondering what to do my friend at the end of the room gave me the thumbs-up sign.

Greeting came at last, pertinent if uneffusive. 'How did you get past, it's not visiting hour?'

'They know me,' I said. 'At least they know Dad.'

'Then find out when I can go.' The dark eyes turned towards me.

'Martin, I am sorry about this,' I said penitently. 'I feel it was my fault.'

'Fiddlesticks. Let's keep to the point. If they know you for God's sake get some information. Better still, take me out.'

'Now wait,' I said cautiously. 'I don't even know what's wrong with you.'

'Nothing. The X-rays were clear.'

'Miss!' Another patient was catching my eye and beckoning. 'I can tell you, miss. It's paralysis. He lost the use of himself.'

When I glanced back terrorstruck Martin had raised himself on an elbow. 'If you don't belt up you'll find I can still use my boot.'

Horrors! My hair stood on end. 'Martin!' I begged.

The informant, a weasel-like man with merry eyes, improved the position by putting up his fists.

'Take no notice of him,' Martin said, mercifully in a more friendly tone.

'Wait now,' the other persisted. 'Let me tell the wee girl. They were taking pictures of him, miss, until three o'clock this morning. I was awake when they brought him in.'

'It was just my arm,' Martin explained cursorily. 'It's all right now.' He went to raise it, got it a few inches off the blanket and broke off, sweat beading his brow.

I made a futile dab at his hand. 'Please. You'll hurt yourself.' My heart pounded with distress and self-recrimination. Innocent or not, I was the cause of this.

'Then get me either the M.O. or my clothes,' he challenged. 'I can't afford to lie here all day answering personal questions.'

It was wilful, reckless, mad. 'From the looks of you, you

can't afford not to,' I retorted. 'Thank goodness *I* don't have to nurse you!'

The atmosphere all but crackled. I stuck my chin out, Martin seemed to crouch back like a panther. If he had hissed it would hardly have surprised me. Then, as swiftly as it had boiled, my anger cooled. 'I'm sorry,' I said shortly. 'That was uncalled-for. I'm not all that hopeful, but I'll do my best.'

There was an odd little pause. Martin's eyes were velvet. The deceivers of the spectrum, that's what brown eyes are.

'It's years since I apologized,' he stated calmly. 'But I don't mind it in others. And I accept the offer, with complete confidence. Looking like that, what man could resist you?'

It was true I had put my hair up and dressed more formally than usual. Petrol blue herringbone suit with velvet facing, white tie-neck shirt, navy tights and bar shoes, a long rust necklace. One can get sudden urges to look demure – or smart, or gentle, or casual. It's what being a woman is about and it does not imply looking for male approval. Nevertheless, I blushed.

'Charming,' he said, and for once he sounded sincere.

I was not required to be irresistible. A close friend of our family, in fact my godfather, had a senior appointment on the hospital staff. When he had recovered from the surprise of seeing me he told me all I needed to know.

Martin had been lucky. There was no 'structural damage', though at first they had suspected a ruptured spleen and he had spent three hours in X-ray. His spine had been badly jarred and he had torn muscles. All these would mend quite quickly. 'The guy has grit,' my godfather concluded. 'I was rough with him, of course. Can't have every Tom, Dick or Harry thinking they can drive fifteen miles with a useless right arm.'

Martin's sentence was short. If all went well he could leave hospital on Sunday. 'But not driving himself. I suppose you'll see to that.'

When I telephoned St. Keir with my findings, Dad's reaction was so prompt that I guessed he and Hew had been doing their homework. Clare had been in touch with the airline. There was a flight Monday forenoon.

It was the obvious time to tell him that I was not going, but the name sidetracked me. 'Clare?' I echoed.

'Oh – Clare Weston, Martin's assistant,' he filled in.

At least I had verified her existence. I wished it was possible to ask how she had taken the news of the accident. I had a feeling, however, that the little Martin had told me had been in confidence. There could be no harm, though, in asking if Dad had met her.

'Yes. A charming girl,' he answered at once. 'Did he tell you about her? She's a widow. Lost her husband last year and went back to work. Martin thinks the world of her. She's very good for him, takes a lot of the strain. But we're not talking about Clare now, we're talking about you two. Can we expect you on Monday?'

I knew he would never forgive me if I let Martin travel alone. And there was still the inescapable truth that but for my keepsake none of this would have happened.

'I'll ring to confirm it,' I replied. 'But I should think so.'

The next two days had pace. By Saturday morning Martin had joined 'Mr. Weasel's' card school, by Saturday night he was downstairs watching television. On Sunday afternoon he was discharged.

I picked him up and we got a royal send-off. Martin kissed one of the nurses and the ward cheered him to a man. I watched incredulously, it was so out of keeping with the smooth arrogant man I knew. The surprises didn't end there. We had to stop at a tobacconist's and sweet shop and have a parcel made up for delivery to the ward. Martin took a business card from a monogrammed wallet and while I goggled crossed out: 'Mr. M. M. Trelawney' and wrote 'Lord Charles'.

'They called me that,' he explained.

'I think you enjoyed yourself,' I marvelled.

He admitted that it had been 'an experience', in the same category as boarding school. When I made the time-honoured jibe about the happiest days of his life, he said quite seriously: 'They were. I loved school. I was quite sorry to leave.'

I would have dearly loved to know more. Where had he gone to school? What games had he played? What subjects had he enjoyed most? I don't think I had ever thought of him as a person until that moment. And of course a person had first to be a child, and that was dangerous because I gave my heart to practically everything that was small or defenceless and they all tore it . . . dogs and cats without number, a cock, a horse, and now, just possibly, a little boy with chocolate button eyes who had found at school the happiness his home had not given him. I knew his parents had separated many years ago.

'Have dinner with me,' Martin invited as I dropped him at the Abyssinian where I had reserved a room for him that night.

It might have been wiser to say no.

Life had been hectic for the past few days. I let the tension ooze out of me in a warm bath. I still didn't know whether or not I would say it, but I was content to let the evening decide.

What to wear? I needed to look well but not too formal. In the end I chose a royal blue shirt and a long skirt the same colour but diced in white, chestnut and buttercup. I swirled my hair into a bun, coaxed out a curl or two and selected a rope of beads. The warm evening made a coat unnecessary.

I thought of Hew whom I loved and for whom no fuss was ever required. Martin I did not love, but he was a connoisseur. I had seen it in his eyes. I wouldn't please him by failing to meet his standards.

The Abyssinian had a signboard with a picture of the sleek lion-coloured cat that had given the house its name. They also had the original, fond of cheese, beer and the bar counter.

Martin had suggested that we meet in the bar and when I entered the cat was dozing by a bottle of Vermouth. Martin was playing with its ears. It looked irritated but polite. Martin looked new. He hadn't a change of suit, but he had put on a different tie, the colour of port wine, and a clean shirt with a pink Tattersall check. In a ridiculous way I felt honoured.

59

We each had a gin and tonic. Early on, the cat turned up at our table, snubbing as usual but interested.

'Rather like you,' Martin observed. 'Golden, beautiful and repressing. Not in that order.'

'What order, then?' I asked unwisely.

'Ah!' he tantalized. 'You'd like to know all my secrets. You must leave me one.'

'You have a great many secrets, Martin,' I said sharply. 'You're quite a mysterious person. In that way you also resemble the cat.'

'So!' His hand against the glass was leather brown and slender. 'We could say that we've fused.'

It was a few seconds before I could draw my eyes from the magnet his seemed to contain. To my annoyance I had set up a train of thought that made me blush.

'We could say nothing of the kind! We're not in the least compatible.'

His gaze was still travelling my face. 'I wonder,' he said reflectively.

The next hour could have set me wondering too, except that I sensed Martin was keeping it on a social basis. He was an accomplished host and he had a hungry girl on his hands. I've always had a fondness for the food at the Abyssinian, melon that came off the rind in juicy slivers, lean mild ham with fat peaches and a classy white wine from France that sparked the palate and fully repaid Martin's study of the wine list.

I had been so busy with journey arrangements that I'd lunched off a sandwich and it showed. I left not a single morsel on the plate. The waitress said it was a treat to see and Martin seemed to catch the mood and kept filling my glass.

It was the first time we had talked without sniping at each other. Martin told me about Cornwall, the common ancestry shared by Cornish, Bretons and Irish and the fascinating fact that Cornishmen had always got their wealth from the earth – as tinners, quarriers, clay workers and farmers. He promised me my first sight of the china clay region, which he said was like the mountains of the moon.

From there it was a natural step to pottery. Martin

asked if I had ever tried decoration. He was walking a knife edge and he knew it, but he was careful to keep the conversation general. In fact he was interesting and predictably practical, telling me what made a design good from a commercial aspect and how decoration for tableware should always be in harmony with food.

There was nothing particularly new in this. I had heard it at art school. But his phrases were crisp and pungent and he backed them with examples.

It was a field I had never considered; rightly or wrongly, I always saw myself drawing pictures.

'Isn't that the trouble, Judy?' he challenged suddenly. 'It's time you gave up meditating and went into production.'

'I've explained . . .' I began edgily.

'Indeed. And I agree – but not for this length. If your stuff is any good it should have been keeping you long ago.' He added cruelly: 'You must decide your priorities. If it's travel – fine, carry on. If you want to be an artist – work at it. Get yourself a studio, knock on doors, don't get sidetracked. That's happened, hasn't it? Just as it did with Hew.'

'Let's leave Hew out of this,' I clipped. 'Say what you like about me, you're probably right.' I couldn't deny that there had been moments when I'd looked down at my typewriter and asked myself: 'Should I be doing this?' nor that such moments had occurred more frequently of late, nor that basically I seemed to have got cold feet about my chosen profession. But Hew was different. He was a true artist – look at the Isolde.

'I am looking at her,' Martin said gently. 'She still has a lot of that mousse on her plate. Don't you want it?'

'Mm, mm,' I answered inelegantly. Heaven knows what it was doing to my waistline; it was chocolate, terribly rich, terribly creamy, terribly good. And I was having it, every last bit.

He waited smiling while I scooped up the final mouthful and then we moved from the dining-room to have coffee in a corner of the lounge. It had been a wonderful meal. Martin had been diplomatic, we had kept off dangerous topics and I was lazy and replete.

I enjoy black coffee, it always seems a civilized part of dinner, but now as I sipped it I remembered what had been in my head setting out. 'Oh lord, I haven't said anything,' I thought.

'When did you last see Hew?' Martin asked abruptly.

I thought. 'About four years.'

'Yes.' Again he seemed to be appraising me. 'He'll find you more beautiful than ever.'

'Thank you,' I said uncertainly. 'Can you understand that that sort of thing isn't important between Hew and me?' I watched his head shake. His mouth wore a curve of amusement, his eyes were sombre. 'We're . . .'

'Soulmates?'

'Something like that.' In the past few days I had been thinking more and more about Hew. Martin's question on Wednesday night had been intrusive but disturbing. Would I marry Hew if he asked me? I'd suffered enough, dear knows, just thinking of what Iceberg had done to him. And though I wasn't a gadabout my social life for the past seven or eight years had been adequate. I'd met plenty of lads that I liked, but none for whom I would give up my independence. Hew was a part of me already. It would be a lovely thing to take care of him and make him happy. All in all, the mix seemed just about right.

'Be sure it's enough.' Martin might have been a mind-reader. 'Don't confuse a rolypoly kid with a woman. You now have – appetite.'

'Which is no concern of yours!' Strange that I didn't feel angry.

'Acknowledged with regret,' he said, smiling. 'But I know how emotional decisions can bring tragic consequences. Though even that, I suppose, is better than no decision at all.'

Did he know he had sighed? I fancied not. It had been almost inaudible. A man as domineering as Martin would think sighing weakness.

My thoughts turned at once to Clare who was 'making no decision at all', presumably because she had been through the trauma of bereavement and was afraid of caring and suffering again.

'I think we have a ghost with us,' Martin said suddenly. 'And three's a crowd. More coffee?' He lifted the pot with a noticeable effort. I watched covertly, knowing he would hate me to comment. Our eyes met and I glanced away.

That arm, I felt sure, was still giving him pain.

'Thank you for coming tonight,' he added. 'Feeling as you do about me, it was quite a gesture.'

'I enjoyed it very much,' I said. 'I . . .' The atmosphere had a strange quality and I felt childishly that the whole room was listening.

'Yes?' Martin invited politely. He was smiling.

I drew a breath and said it in one go. 'When we go to Cornwall, if you still want, I will pretend we're engaged.'

It had an effect I had not quite expected. The first absolute stillness in Martin's face was followed by a warmth I felt I should not look at.

'Why?' he asked.

'Try telling me,' I cornered. 'Something to do with Clare, I thought.'

'Oh!' He looked at me, lips folded. 'It wouldn't be my arm at all, would it? Because that's no reason. If you think an account can always be cleared you're wrong. There's more to life than the balance of payments, take the word of an expert.'

Annoyed, I waxed defensive. 'And if I am trying to pay my debt to you, what's wrong with that?'

'It's not wrong. Just impossible. There is no debt,' he said shortly. 'Besides, you'd find my fiancée an exacting part. On second thoughts I don't think you'd be up to it. Your heart wouldn't be in it.'

'You're quite absurd, Martin.' The effect of the dinner was still with me. I was too comfortable to be angry. 'Of course my heart is not in question. How could it be? My head is a much better bet, that's what I'm offering you. On the count of three, take it or leave it, I don't mind.'

He nodded resignedly. 'Unfeminine and unflattering, but doubtless your first time. I accept. Give me your hand.'

Somehow I had not expected this. It seemed a shame. I

put my hand out and he took it. The gesture that had slipped the signet off his own finger had been brisk, he fitted it on mine slowly and gently. 'Best I can do at short notice.'

'Do I need it at all? It's cheating.' I looked down, hot-cheeked. 'Especially this way. That's a family ring.'

The crest on the signet was that of a knight's helm. Inscribed round the inside of the ring were the words 'Re e merito'. My Latin was not good enough, so he translated. 'Act worthily'. There was a touch of black comedy about it when you considered Haresmead and the eviction of Hew. All I can say is that Hew tumbled into mind. I could almost feel him reproaching me. Not in words, he would never do that, but in a certain quietness that I had just begun to notice in him before I had gone away. He was so understanding, however, that I didn't doubt, once I explained, he would sympathize and even lend support.

'You must brief me about Clare,' I said as Martin escorted me to the car. 'Tomorrow will be time enough, but I must have the complete picture.'

'We'll talk about it,' he promised. 'In the meantime thank you. I shall do my best to make you happy.'

'You needn't joke about it,' I said sharply.

What happened next was confusing. One minute I was standing there twiddling the car keys, the next Martin's sound arm had drawn me to him and he was kissing my mouth. It was a hard kiss, utterly sure of itself.

'I'm very serious – Isolde,' he told me softly. 'Aren't you?'

CHAPTER FIVE

NEXT day we exchanged the pink and white hedges of may round Dublin Airport for the honeysuckle and tamarisk of Cornwall. In between there had been blue silk sea, a bitten sandy coast, Exeter where we had had lunch, the long miles across Dartmoor to the border, Brown Willy rising from Bodmin Moor and now the stark stone building of Jamaica Inn.

It was my first sight of smugglers' Cornwall. There were to be others.

A somewhat menacing face with a patch over one eye looked down at me from the blackened timber of the signpost and gave me a silly feeling of apprehension. Smugglers were above all secret men. I had thrown in my lot with such a man and there had been moments when I had bitterly regretted the whole thing. Last night's extraordinary comment after we had kissed had kept sleep away from me for a long time.

How dared Martin draw meanings from a kiss about which I had no option? Of course I was not serious – any more than he was.

It had been a relief when I called at the Abyssinian this morning with Mrs. Burns, who was driving us to the airport, to find that last night's Martin had vanished with the smart business suit. Today's Martin in red sweater and a red and white check shirt had been a good companion, pleasantly relaxed.

I made myself laugh at the smuggler on the inn sign, but was glad just the same to leave him behind.

Martin was intrigued by my eagerness to get going. 'What's the matter? I thought you'd like a drink. It's a long time since lunch.'

'Some place not so grim,' I parried.

Bodmin sat on a hill. There was a blue heat haze and great carmine splodges of rhododendron. Wadebridge below it, at the head of the Camel estuary, was a pleasant market town. The names on the signposts began to look really Cornish, Trebetherick, Polzeath, Pendogget.

'By "Tre", "Pol" and "Pen" you will know the Cornishmen,' Martin informed me. 'Not far now,' he added. 'But first I'm going to buy you that drink.'

His gaze rested for a minute on my hands, as indeed they had been doing ever since Exeter. I was well aware of this and a little chagrined. I was a perfectly good driver and quite capable of handling the car.

We were no more than four miles from St. Keir and I was all agog to see Dad and Hew, so the suggested stop was irksome. I said nothing, however, and turned obediently down a side road when instructed.

This inn, I had to admit, was charming and not in the least grim. It was whitewashed with a thatched porch, bullseye window glass and a little apron of white cobbles and paintbox-bright flowerbeds. Inside, the focal point was a huge dog grate, glowing redly and setting off the items grouped round it, bellows, a copper pan and jug, horse brasses, a warming pan and an antique china dish.

Martin carried our drinks past a pair of hames and a brass warming pan. The building was sixteenth-century with ships' timbers amongst its ceiling beams. The grate I had already noticed. Martin drew my attention to the slate floor and the old cloam oven. The inn, he added, had once been used by smugglers and there was supposed to be a secret passage from it to the river.

Fortunately this was not on view. Friends had once taken me caving in Yorkshire and we had lost the way back to the entrance. Inwardly I had been hysterical by the time we got back to the daylight. It was some time ago, but the memory was still painful.

'Now will you tell me about Clare?' I had not liked to press a delicate subject, but time was running out and I needed to do my homework.

'What did you want to know?' he countered. 'You'll like her. Everyone does.'

'She's a widow?' I probed.

He looked a little surprised. 'Yes. Her husband died last year after a long illness. He was our chief shape designer, it was a tragic business. But Clare was a trojan. She never let him down.'

I took the change in his voice for emotion. 'I can tell you're very fond of her,' I said softly.

'Very,' he answered shortly.

'Then it would be well not to overdo this plot,' I warned. 'I know you think she'll fight me for you, but there's just a chance she might not. As a woman myself I can understand the battle her pride will give her.'

'But she's not a scrap like you,' Martin returned flatly.

It made my back feel suddenly cold.

'May I top you up?' he suggested.

I shook my head hurriedly. 'No, thanks. Let's move on.'

It was not a propitious beginning. I had known I was not the prototype of love, but he could have been less decisive.

'First things first,' he was now declaring. 'Put your ring on.' As I looked blank his expression changed. 'What's up? You haven't left it behind?'

It explained the searching way he had been looking at my hand, nothing to do with my driving as I had thought. That at least was mollifying.

'Of course not. It's in my bag.' As he seemed to be waiting for something I added: 'Clare won't be there to-night, will she? I want to tell Dad and Hew first.'.

'I've already done so,' he said casually. 'Your father seems quite pleased.'

Something about the eyes sent my heart into my throat. 'What did you tell Dad?'

'That we're engaged.' Martin's gaze was unflickering. 'I proposed a few days ago. You accepted me last night. We have no immediate plans for the wedding.'

'But you can't have . . .' The world took a crazy lean. 'It's not the truth. I mean . . . *Martin*!' Adding insult to injury, he had left me and was walking to the bar counter.

I didn't want another drink – it would have choked me. I demanded this travesty put right. Martin was brutally quiet. 'Those are the facts, Judith. They're what we give to the world. And that includes everyone, even your father and Hew.'

'Hew?' I could not bear it if Hew were to believe this treachery.

'Especially Hew,' Martin said evenly. 'Judith, what did you expect, girl? A charade with everyone knowing the game except Clare? How long would that last, I ask you? Be reasonable.'

'I could say: Be honourable,' I flashed. 'But that's impossible, I know.'

'If you like to think so,' he said, unmoved.

I had no answer, so I stayed silent. The fresh glasses he had brought stood on the table between us. I wondered if it was the bright red sweater and the open shirt that gave him a piratical air. Dark. Swarthy. Cruel. Above all deep. No smuggler had ever trodden a more hidden path. What a fool I'd been to weaken, what a crass, blind fool.

'I hate you,' I said.

'Well, that doesn't make a change,' he returned easily. 'You always have. Drink up and we'll get going.'

'I'm not sure I want to – now.'

'Oh, come on.' He looked amused. 'If I've swept you off your feet you were always susceptible to emotion. Your father will understand and forgive you.'

'How dare you!' I gasped. 'You have *not* swept me off my feet. I contracted an honourable payment, and you took advantage.'

A change came to Martin's face. All at once it looked cold. 'I think this mud-slinging has gone far enough. Stop it or stop the engagement. You'll remember I had doubts about your professionalism; it seems they were justified.'

'You mean you won't hold me to it?' I asked uncertainly.

'At this moment it would be a pleasure to let you go.'

It was release. I knew that before long I would feel joy and relief. My immediate reaction was stupefaction. 'Then it's off . . .'

'If that's what you want. There are some games not worth the candle,' he said steadily. 'Have your drink and we'll go.' He lifted his own glass and tasted it.

I felt very quiet as I followed suit. Quiet and small. As though, unfair as it was, I was the one who had failed.

Martin gave me an unexpected smile. 'All right, no hard feelings. You can pick the lilies.'

'I beg your pardon?' I stuttered.

The smile changed to a light laugh. 'Sorry. It's a song. You don't know it?'

To my astonishment he began to sing, softly and as unselfconsciously as years ago in Hew's sitting-room.

    ' "Oh, you will pick the lilies
        And I'll pick the thyme,
    And you will drink to your love,
        And I'll drink to mine!" '

Nature had given him a most sympathetic voice and me a wild heart. I struggled madly. I hated this man. He had taken away from me so much that I loved. If in turn I was blocking his chance of happiness it was only an eye for an eye. Why should I care? I didn't.

I don't suppose the agony lasted more than a minute, but it seemed like eternity plus. Everything passed through my mind, not excepting the clear pain after Prince had been killed. I hated grief. I hated it objectively. I even hated it for my enemy.

My enemy. He looked me back as steadily. He did not plead. I knew that this round was mine and suddenly I could not bear the victory.

If this had been a duel I would have given him the chance to pick up his sword. Heaven knows why – and heaven wasn't telling – but I opened my handbag and took out the ring. The words *'Re e merito'* looked up at me from inside the band.

'My head is all I'm offering you,' I said clearly. 'Remember that.'

If my surrender surprised him he gave no sign. As I realized later he did not even thank me.

'Gladly,' he said briefly. 'If you'll also remember that you've taken my ring.'

It would be impossible to say exactly what I had expected Chards to be like, something out of the country house department of a West End store with a rustic name board. In fact, it displayed no name at all. It was an old house tucked in the angle of a lane. Far from hitting the eye with new brick, it hid in its little green orchards.

I was too excited at the thought of seeing Dad to notice much more than that. Martin ran the car on to the drive and opened the door for me. The house was oblong with a glass verandah and deep blue paint. The garden was oldfashioned with tall flowers. I saw nothing in detail except the dear figure that had come through the verandah door and was holding out its arms.

Two seconds later I was in them.

'I don't know,' Dad said affectionately. 'You've been talent-spotting three continents for five years and five days did it in the end. Must be love. Where is the brave man? Let me tell him what he's in for.'

'No need, sir,' Martin had joined us, smiling. 'He's known for seven years.'

It was hair-raising.

'Delighted, lad,' my father was saying, wringing his prospective son-in-law's hand. 'And so would Mary have been. I wish she could have known.'

'Perhaps she does,' Martin suggested, slipping his hand through my arm. 'One would like to think so.'

'Aye.' It was fortunate Dad was not looking at my face. I was fuming. Need Martin do everything with such consummate skill? It would make it all the harder for my father when the pretence was over. I had somehow not bargained for the degree of his pleasure.

Thank goodness he looked very fit. I could see he had lost weight, but he was tanned and still had his twinkle.

'Good to see you, love,' he whispered as we all walked into the house. 'Just what the doctor needed.'

'Now is it my turn?' a voice asked whimsically from the hallway. Hew! It was a painful moment. I swung round, bracing myself. Angry or hurt, he would be hard to meet.

Happily he seemed to be neither. He was smiling, he looked brown and well fed, his hair was trimmed and his 'country and western' shirt was very smart. My heart turned over with joy. 'Hew! How lovely!'

'Judy, let me look at you!' He caught me with a chuckle and hugged me tight. 'He's not getting away with this, you know. You were always mine.' He kissed me again, not once but many times. I found myself making an embarrassed protest.

'Well, that's what you get for doing the dirty on me,' Hew declared. 'I'll see you in my study after school.'

'After that I don't think you'll see me for dust!' I joked shakily.

The almost hectic warmth of the greeting had been

disturbing, I couldn't deny it, but neither could I deny that the meeting had gone far better than I'd feared.

Martin's arm was still not good enough for carrying cases, so Dad brought my bag up to the bedroom which had been allotted me. It was on the front of the house, the middle one of the three which topped the verandah. I liked the room – it was simple with white walls, a canary yellow bedcover and black and white flowered curtains – but I liked the view from it even more.

The garden was straight off a calendar, gay and bushy with flowers each side of a wide path.

The bouquet of fresh cut grass wafted up to me. To the right, over one orchard, was the spire of a church; to the left, over the other orchard, was surely blue sea. This was something with which Dunbeagle could not compete.

Dad, watching my delight, confirmed the assumption. We were looking down the estuary to the coast; Polzeath on the point had some of the best surfing in the north of the country. 'Only a few minutes' drive. Martin might take you after dinner.'

'Dad, how is Hew really?' I asked as he was about to leave me. 'I got such a shock when I found out about Iceberg.'

'Aye, I knew you would. That's why I hadn't got round to telling you,' he admitted. 'But Hew's fine, I think. Don't you worry about him.'

There was still much I wanted to know, but time forbade it. Mrs. Trigg, Martin's housekeeper, was a dragon where unpunctuality for meals was concerned. She set great store by her cooking; tonight in celebration of Martin's homecoming, we were to have roast duck and all afternoon Dad and Hew had been hearing warnings that it would go dry if kept waiting.

I had no desire to make an enemy on my first night, so I didn't dawdle. I had few enough dresses, but the importance of first night duck seemed to demand one. My choice was striped with a soft black leather belt. It was dead plain with long sleeves and a stand-up collar, but the stripes were in unusual colours, mauve and violet, sherry, sand and dark green.

I brushed my hair out and took its top piece higher on

my head, rummaged in my case for gilt chains which were a constant standby and risked a sienna blusher that brought up the subtler shades in the dress. I hoped Martin would approve because it was a look he would see over and over again – on most occasions, in fact, when a dress was called for.

Then I went downstairs to the duck, which had after all waited with an exceptionally good grace.

Dad's plans were for a three-week holiday. He had arrived a week ago and would be returning to Dunbeagle on the last day of the month. It was exactly a fortnight away and I hoped it would also serve as a time limit for my ordeal.

'Well, what do you think of Chards?' Martin asked suddenly.

'What I've seen of it, I love,' I answered sincerely. 'It has a happy feel.'

The phrase was evidently the right one. 'It was owned by a happy man,' he said briefly. 'As Hew will endorse.'

It brought a smile. 'Uncle Richard. Yes,' Hew agreed. 'The happiest of men. We would all have changed shirts with him gladly, but that's never possible, is it?'

My father made no comment, Martin flicked a glance up the table and went on serving. It was I who asked Hew what he meant.

'If you remember the fable,' he said reflectively, 'the king was rich and melancholy. The treatment prescribed was to find a happy man and change shirts with him, but when servants located the only happy man in the kingdom he was found not to possess a shirt.'

I remembered the legend. 'It's very true.'

'It's bunkum,' Martin declared roundly. 'Unless he lived in the tropics, And it in no way relates to Uncle Richard. He may not have been a millionaire, but I'd hardly call him shirtless. What do you think this house would fetch today?'

'I meant metaphorically, of course,' Hew had flushed a little. 'And comparatively. He was not one of our tycoons. The Trelawneys, Judy, produce tycoonery with boring regularity. Look at your future husband.'

I did so and was not reassured. Martin's face was an

oval of pursed lips and cold dark eyes. 'If anyone married me for my money they'd be in for a shock,' he said ominously. 'I'm safe with Judith.'

It was truer than anyone except me realized, but it was also good acting. So was the almost shy smile that followed. If the name of Martin Trelawney ever went up in lights in London's theatreland I could say: 'Here's where it all began.'

'Tell me about your uncle. What did he do?' I asked, embarrassed.

'He was the schoolmaster in St. Keir for forty years. As Hew says, he never made a fortune, but he was comfortable. He had this place and he looked after it, left it as sound as a bell.' The little silence round the table suggested that each of us was thinking of Haresmead. I know I was doing so as Martin went on: 'He was ninety when he died twelve years ago, but he'd become a sort of legend here. It was the thing for all the kids to visit him, a latter day Mr. Chips if you like, though more of an outdoor type.'

'Indeed,' Hew agreed readily. 'You'd have loved him, Judy. He used to paint a bit too. Some of the pictures inside are his. We must show you.'

Again I thanked my stars that it was not in Hew to show disappointment or harbour a grudge.

'Any messages?' Martin asked as Mrs. Trigg brought in the sweet.

'Clare was looking for you,' Hew replied. 'There's a flap on with the union.'

'Did she say what about?' Martin poured cream on his fruit salad.

Hew said a name, Tom Grundy.

'It would be,' Martin commented.

Clare must have been holding the fort during Martin's absence. How torn she must have felt between him in hospital in Ireland and the trouble brewing at the works. I was very curious about Clare. Not every girl was strong enough to live to herself.

Meantime, it might be well to remember that *I* at the moment was supposed to live as Martin's fiancée. It did not matter that so far as I personally was concerned Iceberg's bothers were no more than their just deserts. I was expected to be involved, I had a duty to care.

'Is it serious?' I asked belatedly.

'Won't know that till I ring,' Martin answered promptly. 'But no one laughs at the union these days.' He stood up. 'Shan't be long. Then I'll take you to Polzeath.'

He was out of the room for longer than I had expected. It set up ridiculous conjecturings. Was the news bad? Was he telling Clare about us? I was almost a non-smoker, but when Hew flicked his case open I took one and drew on it nervily. Dad looked at me and I could see the doctor in him rise to the surface. If he knew the true situation, however, he would understand why I needed to calm myself.

'On a night like this we're bound to see some surfing,' Hew remarked. 'We'll use my car, though. You've had enough driving for one day.'

His unfailing thoughtfulness and kindness brought a lump to my throat.

But at that moment Martin's head came round the door. 'Judy! Where are you? Come and have a word with Clare.'

Such was my state of mind that I almost jumped out of my skin.

'Come on, she won't bite,' he said, laughing, and hustled me across the hall.

She didn't. My first impression of Clare Weston was her pleasant voice. It was warm and friendly and it sounded incredibly genuine. 'Judy? I hope you don't mind my asking for you. Martin told me your news and I did want to wish you well.'

I could see the bloom of heat on the telephone from my hand. Silly to get so worked up, but I loathed pretence.

'How very nice of you, thanks,' I said uncertainly.

Clare hoped she would see me soon. No doubt Martin would be showing me the plant. I gave her a guarded 'yes'. I would cross that bridge when I had to.

For all the miles that the day had put between myself and Haresmead, at that moment I saw it clearly, the felled trees, the levelled cottage and the green hill waiting to be gashed. All by order of the monster Iceberg. After all, nothing had changed. Nothing had healed the pain.

My reply must have sounded abstracted, for I saw Martin glance at me and in a couple of seconds his hand closed over the telephone. 'Sorry to cut in, Clare, but I don't like the sound of this Grundy thing. Could you spare me an hour if I went over?' Clare must have assented, for he said briskly: 'Right. See you,' and the phone clicked back in its cradle.

I thought for the minute that he was going to castigate me. His look had been so keen, almost like an X-ray machine, and I was certain his ear had picked up the mechanical tone in which I had spoken to Clare. It was a surprise and relief when he said quite gently: 'That's my evening washed out, I'm afraid. Not to worry, we can see Polzeath any time.'

It struck me suddenly that he looked very tired.

Clare lived in Wadebridge, four miles away, and Martin insisted that he could drive himself over. My father thought otherwise. In the end after some skirmishing he won. 'Don't argue. I'm doing the driving. I know, I know, you'll both be talking shop. What about it? I can take the dog for a walk.'

This was a saying of Dad's. I was not sure whether or not Clare possessed a dog.

'What about Judy?' Martin protested. 'You won't want to leave her on her first night.'

'Sure, what about her?' Dad returned like any true father. 'She can either keep or come with me.'

I wanted to say: 'Oh no!' The past hour had been one hurdle after another. Clare would be a most difficult one and I was too much on edge to face her at the moment.

There was a pause, infinitesimal I supposed, but awkward. As I opened my mouth I caught Martin's eye. It seemed like a sort of sheet anchor. I felt quite suddenly that I could leave it to him.

'Let her put her feet up,' he said smoothly. 'If that's all right?' As I nodded gratefully he went on: 'I know Clare wants to meet you, darling, but Tom Grundy comes first, I'm afraid. We have a lot to think about.'

'Including the fact that last Thursday you could have

broken your back,' Dad remarked dryly. 'You take it easy, lad. You're not made of steel.'

'Blame inflation for that!' Martin flashed. 'They could only afford the heart.'

It was considerably more typical than the endearment. A good try, no doubt, but Martin calling me 'darling' had sounded as odd as two left feet. And yet how intuitive he had been, how quickly he had got the message that I was in no shape to meet Clare tonight.

Unless, of course, he had not wanted my presence any more than I had wanted to be there. Did I believe Tom Grundy would be the sole topic discussed? Martin loved Clare, Clare loved Martin if she could dare to admit it. Martin had turned *provocateur* to bring this about. From this moment on he would be playing a double game. In company he would give a faultless portrayal of my fiancé, in private with the girl he loved he would have to let her see that old fires could be rekindled.

At least that was the way I saw it, and very tired I was. It hadn't been quite what I'd expected. I knew Dad was pleased to see me, but he had actually made more fuss of Martin.

One had to be adult about things, but suddenly I was lonely. I think the honeysuckle had something to do with it. It was all through the hedge and it was so sweet that it made me want to cry.

I was still standing in the garden when Hew came out. 'Here you are. I've been looking for you. Let's go for a drive.'

'A drive?' He had caught me unawares and I felt stupid.

'Yes, why not?' he challenged. 'It might be raining tomorrow.' Another thing about him that had not changed was the wide lopsided smile that always made him look in need of care and protection.

'All right,' I said, laughing. 'May I order? Sea, please.'

'One sea, bright and beautiful, comin' right up!' he promised.

The bay at Polzeath was all of that. The sea was the colour of Isolde's gown in Hew's picture, the sands were beaten gold. As the long lazy rollers creamed over them it was a love affair. There were several people with surfboards, some with the marlin spikes which Hew said were permitted after seven, and a couple of schoolgirls on ponies were walking them along the margin.

My pleasure kept me silent. I was utterly entranced. I could do something with this view, not exactly a painting. My canvases, as I knew to my cost, were too like photographs. What I wanted here was to catch the lovemaking of the sea – and the inevitability. The sand shone like any girl in love but without the storms of despair. It had to happen, I thought, mesmerized. The sea had to come back, they had to be together.

It may have been the connection of colours that brought Isolde so vividly to mind. Isolde who should have hated and could not, Isolde who could not escape her love and in the end had died because of it.

'It's lovely,' I said inadequately.

'It is indeed,' Hew responded with his eyes on my face. 'The wine is fully matured.'

'Oh, Hew!' I was feeling so far from mature that it was laughable. 'You're so good at picking up pieces.'

A twist came to his mouth. 'I should have thought I'm far better at letting them lie.'

As I turned my head inquiringly he flushed. 'Judy, what is this madness?'

'I'm not sure I know what you mean,' I said awkwardly.

'In other words shove off. I'm damned if I will. Not without knowing what's behind it.'

'If you mean Martin . . .' I looked fixedly at the ring on my finger.

'Yes, I mean Martin – up to his old games, I imagine – taking advantage . . .'

It was typical. Hew had always been a knight errant. Distressed as I felt, my lips began to twitch. 'No, love, nothing like that. He's been in hospital!'

'And I'm not straight from the Ark,' Hew returned angrily. 'And nor are you. You've been four years away and I give you credit . . .'

'What, then?' I interrupted.

77

'Isn't it obvious? You left Sydney because some guy let you down and Martin saw his chance – a nice rebound job. I hand it to him. When it comes to a mopping up operation there's none better.'

I was more bewildered then angered. Hew talking like that was a stranger.

'Perhaps, but not in my case,' I said firmly. 'No one let me down in Australia. I came home to see Dad – there was no other reason. Martin was in Dunbeagle and we got engaged. End of story.'

'No. I don't believe it. You always hated him.' Hew's head shook.

I felt my fingers close on the signet. The lettering inside the band seemed to be burning through. '*Re e merito*'. '*Act worthily*'. Martin's voice echoed: 'If you'll also remember that you've taken my ring.'

'It was a long time ago when I hated him. Attitudes change.'

'Judy, look at me,' Hew commanded. 'Can't you see? I love you. I can't let him get away with it.'

'It's not a question of getting away with it,' I said patiently. 'It takes two to make an engagement.'

'But did you hear what I said? he demanded. 'I love you. And you love me, Judy. Let me convince you.'

'Hew,' I implored, 'you did – all of twelve years ago. I'm not afraid to say it. I do love you.'

'Like a brother, I suppose?' The sneer was hurtful.

'I wouldn't know about that,' I reminded him. 'We never ran to one. And it's no use, I can't analyse these things. If I go deeper in I'll hurt you more. You're all my happy things, love. Leave it at that.' The words strung together so easily that it seemed someone else had done the thinking.

I looked at him wordlessly and with an aching heart.

Next minute his arm went round me and his hand touched my cheek and began caressing my hair. Kisses followed, quick and greedy. I don't think he even noticed that they were not being returned. I certainly did not realize that I was crying until a tear splashed on to my nose.

Hew's grasp of me slackened. He gave me a harassed

smile and I said the first thing that came into my head.

'It was such fun when we used to watch the badgers.'

It had a strange effect. Hew sat looking at me in silence.

'You're very clever,' he said at last. 'But not clever enough, if you think you and Martin will ever be happy together.'

There was no answer to that. I sat silent watching the sea.

'I'm sorry, Judy, I can see you're angry,' Hew said awkwardly.

'No. Just tired,' I assured him.

But it was more than that. Something had knocked the stuffing out of me.

CHAPTER SIX

DAD and Martin were not back when we reached home, so I was able to excuse myself and go to bed. Next morning when I went downstairs my father was in the hall eavesdropping shamelessly on a telephone conversation which Martin was having. Martin, I noted, was wearing a dark grey suit and his briefcase was lying on the table.

'Haven't you any control over this man of yours?' Dad challenged.

'Absolutely none,' I said truthfully.

Martin lifted flex and receiver out of the way to kiss me, expertly as always. ''Morning, darling. Pardon the lines of communication. This is a mayday call.'

Obviously not the first time he had handled bird and telephone simultaneously. Practice, I had to admit, had made perfect, and I liked his aftershave.

'Is it the union again?' I asked, carefully intelligent.

Of the three of us Dad was the only non-actor. He was his goodhearted growly self as he tried to persuade Martin to take a breather. I pretended interest as Martin explained that the union troubles were only part of it. His 'production guy' was on leave and they had had a telex to say that two big customers from France were coming over. 'Normally David would lay on the entertaining, but in his absence I've got to be available. I'm really sorry, darling. Can you amuse yourself? Use my car, Jack,' he added, switching back to Dad. 'You could take her to Truro.'

'Darling' again, and sounding much more natural. Not to be outdone, especially with Dad's eye on me, I urged him not to overdo things.

'Remember what they told you at the hospital.'

'All I remember about hospital is how to play poker,' he retorted.

The works were sending a car for him and it came soon after. With obvious tact my father made himself scarce.

'Don't work too hard,' I bade Martin dutifully.

'Walk out to the car with me,' he returned, putting his hand under my elbow.

I thought mischievously: 'Didn't he do well?' Somehow this morning I felt in better form.

The driver, neatly uniformed, said: 'Good morning, sir,' and opened the door. It was impressive, even if the back seat did lack a telephone. I put my head inside to check.

'Now what?' Martin asked patiently.

'No phone,' I said, feigning astonishment. 'Darling, have you thought? For all of half an hour they won't be able to reach you. Will they survive?'

'You mightn't if we were alone,' he told me grimly. In precisely the same breath he added: 'I understand you went to Polzeath last night with Hew. Please don't do that again unless I accompany you.'

The caressing tone made it doubly hard to credit that the face above the pale pink shirt and tie was serious. He really was giving me a warning. How dared he?

'Steady, my love.' The hand on my elbow firmed itself. 'He's watching us. Thinking, I have no doubt, that the boss is a good picker.'

'I'm not joking, Martin. Please take your hand away,' I murmured.

His voice became as silky as the dark wing on his forehead.

'I'll let you go, little dove, when I'm sure you know the

way home.' As I caught my breath in annoyance he kissed my cheek. 'You'll enjoy Truro,' he said in his normal tones. 'I wish I were coming with you.'

Few of my days had ever had such a disturbing start, but as though to compensate the rest of this one was peaceful. In Dad's company I enjoyed Truro to the full. We had lunch, visited the cathedral and looked at the shops. It was good to be together and we had lots to talk about.

Once or twice I caught him staring at me.

'I suppose a cat can look at a king,' he retorted when I challenged him. 'I.was just thinking how well you look today. I thought last night you were a bit peaky, but this morning it was a treat to see you and Martin together. I kept wishing your mother was with me.'

'This morning was only nonsense,' I deprecated.

'I know, I know. Same sort of nonsense that makes the world go round. And you look the better for it, daughter, that's all I can say.'

I smiled weakly. I was not the first actress to discover that the more you gave yourself to a part the thinner became the divider between shadow and substance.

My father went on to tell me how fond both Mummy and he had grown of Martin as his visits to Dunbeagle during the spring of the year had become more frequent. As the rector's wife had told me, it was Mummy who had written to him out of concern for Hew, who all winter had been withdrawn and morose.

'So it was thanks to Mummy that Haresmead was sold.' It was a big hurdle to cross.

They had deliberately left me in ignorance. I was far away and talking of working my ticket to New Zealand and Japan. They had not expected to see me home for years.

'What the eye doesn't see the heart doesn't grieve for,' Dad said. 'So we didn't tell you. At least that's what we decided before she died, and I kept to it.'

'Dad, who owned Haresmead? Who sold it to Iceberg? How did Martin ferret him out?' I asked querulously.

It earned me a sharp look. 'Now why ask me a thing like that? Ask Martin. I'm surprised you haven't already.'

'We don't agree on Haresmead,' I said shortly.

Dad gave me a very direct look. 'Well, I can't tell you because I don't know. And I hope you won't make a fuss. Remember if it hadn't been for Iceberg you wouldn't have got your man!'

Next day Martin was still involved with his French visitors. The car came for him as on Tuesday, but this time he made a businesslike and hasty departure.

As I walked back through the hall after waving him off I stopped to examine an oak chest which stood inside the door. Black with age, it was hard to see it properly, but it was beautiful, heavily and intricately carved. Soon I was kneeling on the floor tracing the lettering so that it made words.

It was a wedding chest. I spelled out the name John Trelawney and that of his bride Susan Maybole. Susan had come from Truro, John from Bodmin. There was the year, 1575, and below it the words: 'Comfort ye one another'.

I hoped they had done so as I got up from my knees. The injunction was a simple one, but it said much and without undue sentiment.

Already I could pinpoint Chard's Cornish features. The rich cobalt blue of its woodwork and guttering. Its glass front. Its 'Jack and Jill' wall – drystone with a her-ringbone pattern.

A watercolour of it painted by its late owner hung in the sitting-room and I had been studying it. Apart from the love which had obviously gone into every line, it showed Chards in the bloom of youth. The garden was a sight to behold, the house was trim and new, the paint glossy and a softer hue. Strange that I should find myself so involved with it and with the man who, unlike John and Susan, had lived here all alone. He had loved chil-dren, but he had never had the joy of a wife and family.

Perhaps in leaving the place to Martin he had hoped to see it revitalized. I thought of Clare with the pleasant voice. If it brought a happy family to Chards then this crazy scheme would have been a bonaventure.

Mrs. Trigg was going out so we had an early lunch and Dad and Hew went to play golf. It was another amazing change; in Dunbeagle Hew had never shown the slightest interest in golf. Now I learned that in the past his handicap had been scratch.

I could have gone with them, but I had awakened with an idea for a design in my head and wanted to sketch it out.

The design was based on the bay at Polzeath, though by the time I had translated it into Arabian arabesques it was doubtful whether anyone but myself would perceive the central thought. I wished I could paint it to try out the greeny blues and golds in my mind's eye, but without the necessary materials this was impossible.

At that point I can only think that my guardian angel took his eyes off the road. I stood up and rambled round the garden. The watercolour on the sitting-room wall had shown me how it had looked in its heyday and I had not been able to forget it. It had now got to the stage when, remembering Haresmead and the trauma of giving oneself unasked to something one did not own, I should have cut and run. Instead I changed into trousers and tee-shirt and set to work.

At first it was simple weeding. The soil was workable and I made excellent progress. So much so in fact that success went to my head. Against the wall were a few old rose trees, gnarled and unproductive, which should have been dug up years ago. Only that morning I had heard Dad say as much to Hew.

The more I looked at them the more unsightly they appeared and I saw they were keeping the light away from other flowers. There were nearly three hours before dinner, could the time be better employed?

A few minutes later, triumphantly wielding a spade I had found in the garage, I was in business.

I have made wrong decisions in my time, few approached the error I made then. No one had ever told me the strength of old rose roots or the mean way they spread and twisted and pulled and would not snap. I must have wrestled for an hour, almost dropping with heat and weariness and too stubborn to give in. My clothes were sticking to me and my hair kept falling into my eyes, but there was still one devil of a tree in the ground.

'Brute!' I muttered resentfully, putting all my weight on the spade.

They say only a bad workman blames his tools. I just hadn't the muscle to lift that octopus-like root. But there it was mocking my efforts. I put one last pressure on the spade.

There was a horrible crack. The blade stayed embedded but the handle tore away. I had time to think that the sound it made was like a human death throe and then I found myself flat on my back on top of the two thorny bushes which I had managed to dislodge.

Apart from the pain, which was excruciating, I seemed to be anchored. The thorns, I realized, had me in their talons. It did nothing for my health and temper to discover that I could not get up. I made an attempt and said: 'Ouch!'

Simultaneously I heard a car. 'Dad!' I called urgently.

Running feet crunched on the gravel. I tried vainly to turn my head without scratching my cheek. 'I'm over here!'

Next instant a voice said: 'Good grief!' It was the last straw. The tones were not those of my father or Hew and to my sensitive nerves they were not wholly free from amusement.

'Hold still. Don't move,' Martin went on as he dropped to his knees beside me. I had to admit that he had sized up the situation at a glance. 'We'll get you up,' he added. 'Don't struggle.'

My mind which had been beating a hysterical tattoo ... 'I've broken his spade.' 'He'll spoil his suit.' 'I don't want him to know.' ... appended a last crescendo of woe. 'We ... who's we ... not *Clare* ...'

'I think I can manage now,' I said desperately. He had done something to the imprisoning shoots. Perhaps I could wriggle out.

'All right, tear your trousers,' he returned equably, and indeed as I shifted there was an ominous rending sound.

84

In the same moment a new face looked down at me, sunbronzed and most attractive in a frame of dark brown hair. Raw and furious as I was, nothing could blind me to the kindness in the look. 'It's all right, I see what's catching it. It's this branch, Martin. Oh, poor Judy, you must be in agony!'

Had Clare Weston been a different kind of person she would have relished the spectacle of her rival torn, bleeding and dishevelled. I looked my worst. The final humiliation was the flapping seat of my jeans. But Clare was not like that. We went upstairs and she helped me to bathe my cuts and sat on the bed while I changed.

'I'm sorry for bursting in like this, Judy. We got the boys off to Paris earlier than we expected and Martin wanted to get back to you, so I thought I could kill two birds – drive him home and meet you – but . . .'

'But nothing,' I interrupted as she rose to zip up my dress. 'From where I was you seemed to have dropped from heaven.'

My role would have been easier if I had disliked her. If she had been the hard-headed beauty I had expected, I would, strange to say, almost have enjoyed the tactics. Divorce Martin from the context of Dunbeagle and he was an interesting character. Somehow with Clare I knew I was on the losing side.

For one thing she was older than me, perhaps even older than Martin. It meant that their love had already surmounted one obstacle.

When Clare lost her suntan she would need make-up, almost certainly when she was tired it would show. But she had sparkling grey-blue eyes, a marvellous sense of humour and bandbox grooming. Long slim legs set off a sleeveless linen-look dress that I could not believe had been in the day's rat race. It was parchment colour, its sole adornment a copper brooch.

Suddenly I felt superfluous. I seemed to see that the link between Martin and Clare would not break. Whether or not she married him she would not be swayed by any blonde red herring from the Irish Sea.

Martin was in the garden proving to himself that his torn muscles were nearly as good as new. He had gathered the old rose trees into a neat pile.

'I'll pay for the spade,' I said without thinking.

When I saw his face freeze I realized that it was an unnatural offer. Who would exact payment from one's fiancée?

'Good, good,' he drawled. 'I might have taken the plunge long ago if I'd known breakages were covered.'

Oh, cripes! I thought. In front of Clare it was so provocative a remark.

She, however, parried it with incredible cool. 'Not looking at me, I hope?'

'Always,' he said simply.

Not twenty-four hours ago *I* had been ordered to be circumspect where Hew was concerned. Surely sauce for the goose should also be sauce for the gander? There Martin had condemned me unseen, here he was making it plain that his heart was still engaged, however hopelessly.

I knew I had bargained for this, I had fitted it into the scheme of things as an inevitable factor. But abstract thought was different from reality. I had taken a hard decision when I had agreed to wear the Trelawney ring and it was galling to be made feel so early in the game that I was not really of account.

Martin and Clare were now discussing the visiting French buyers. It had apparently been difficult to judge their reactions to next year's designs. Masters of diplomacy, they had given no sign of disappointment and yet Martin was uneasy. It was a new connection and one which Iceberg badly wanted to foster.

One of the art courses I had taken while abroad had traced the history of porcelain decoration. The French I recalled were traditionally fond of a decoration which covered most of the ground. The Rococo style came instantly to mind. We had been taught that badly done it was vulgar, but good Rococo forms were elegant and complex. Use was made of intertwining curves, scrollwork and flourishes. The lids of teapots and tureens were encrusted with porcelain flowers, and the famous Sèvres factory under the protection of Marie Antoinette had the monopoly of gilding and some special

86

blue glazes.

Still, all that would be elementary stuff to any high class designer. I had no wish to invite superiority, even if polite.

'I think I'll go and see if Mrs. Trigg needs any help,' I said.

Against all reason the world seemed a lonely place. I walked across the garden without looking back and as I reached the hall door Hew's car drew up.

However complicated my personal life might be, it had one bright spot – my father, and how well and happy he was looking. Smart too. It was a little sign of bravery, that draughtboard shirt in two shades of soft red. Mummy would have approved the purchase.

'Who won?' I called.

'Need you ask?' Dad chuckled, opening his door.

Hew did not follow suit. He was staring at Clare's car which was parked some distance away. My photographic memory again. For the rest of the night it was to show me his face – troubled as a child's under the brown fringe, the big mouth puckered. 'He's anxious,' I thought. 'He feels she shouldn't be here.'

It was not surprising. Hew did not know the whole story, but he was on my side. Already he questioned the depth of Martin's love for me. Now he was thinking that Clare should not be here. Perhaps she should not have been, but she was, and I liked her. Now she came towards us calling a greeting to my father with whom she was obviously on the best of terms.

'Did you beat him?' she added.

'Now why ask a painful thing like that?' Dad returned. 'I suppose you know the kind of game he plays.'

'If it's any consolation I do – the hard way!' Clare agreed, laughing. 'Neither Henry nor I – Henry was my husband – was ever any match for him. Still we always had fun.' She threw Hew quite an affectionate glance. 'What about giving me my revenge one of these fine days?'

Hew, I thought, need not be uptight on my account. Certainly not over something so minor as a game of golf. Yet he looked so serious standing there, serious and ill at ease.

'Not, of course, if you don't want to.' Clare had sensed the withdrawal. Her colour had risen slightly.

Hew must have realized that unwittingly he had been discourteous, for he too had flushed. 'There's no question of not wanting to. Shall we fix a day?'

Clare said Saturday was her best time and the arrangement was duly made. Shortly afterwards we trooped inside for dinner.

As usual it was delicious. Mrs Trigg had rolled up ham and asparagus in a pancake batter and garnished each serving with tomato and mustard and cress. It was a quick dish and apparently she had substituted it when she had seen 'Mrs. Weston's car.'

'I thought so,' said Clare, laughing. She went on to say that she had recently begged the recipe for a super sweet made out of pancakes with mandarin oranges. 'It's terribly good. I must give it to you. You whip a little ground almond into the cream.'

There was no doubt she had the key even to the heart of Martin's dour housekeeper. Mrs. Trigg, supplying in her turn a way of using the same batter with apples and peaches, was a different person. To tell the truth I felt envious. There was no reason for this. In two weeks I expected to be back in Ireland with no prospect of ever seeing Chards again. Clare, on the other hand, with any luck would one day be mistress here.

Mrs. Trigg brought the coffee tray to the glass verandah. It was a summery setting, especially with the scent of pinks and honeysuckle wafting through the open door. But though it was sound, like all the property, it was still an old gentleman's place. And not very imaginative. I began conjuring up the things that could be done with it. Aquamarine paint, lots of bright cushions, masses of pink geraniums. Was there any way the verandah could be extended to make a full-size sun-room? I thought of heavy Spanish rugs and vivid Spanish lamps. I thought of a dinner party and a table setting that would gather in the copper, the apricot and the gold of sunset.

The truth was that Chards called to me not because it was already beautiful but because I could make it so.

I had been dreaming over the coffee. It was perhaps significant that Mrs. Trigg had set the tray down in front of Clare, who had immediately asked gaily:

'Am I to be mother?'

Now I realized that Martin had tapped my knee. 'Wake up, my love. This will interest you.' He had a roll of documents in his hand. 'We are about to unveil Operation Isolde.'

As I looked stupid Clare put in, 'Irish Iceberg. He always calls it that.'

'Might one ask why?' Hew inquired stiffly.

'Elementary, my dear Watson,' Martin replied. 'It's a love affair between Cornwall and Ireland.'

'Love affair?' I echoed before I could help myself. 'That takes some credence.'

'I've been in love with the idea of an Irish company for years,' he answered mildly. 'Ever since I saw Haresmead, in fact. It was ideal for the purpose.'

'I believe you said as much once,' I owned coldly. 'I hoped you didn't mean it.'

'I never say anything I don't mean.' He appeared to be speaking to the room at large, but it was on me that his eyes rested. 'And like my namesake, Mark of Cornwall, I usually get what I want.'

It had not dawned on me until then that Martin was a form of Mark. King Mark of Cornwall had been the instigator of the marriage alliance between his country and Ireland. Isolde had been commanded by her father to marry him, and Tristan, the Cornish knight who had already killed Isolde's lover in combat, had come from Mark's court to escort her to her new country. With every reason to hate Tristan, Isolde had found herself trapped in a doom love. She had tried to escape it by pouring a cup of poison for Tristan and putting her own lips to the deadly contents, but, unknown to her, a love potion, intended for her wedding night with Mark, had been substituted for the poison and as they drank together the flame of their hopeless love was inexorably fanned. Isolde had married Mark but remained helpless before her love for Tristan. The resulting intrigue had separated them and brought them together again to die tragically at the moment when their pardon was on its way.

'I think you forget Mark's magnanimity at the end,' I challenged sharply.

There was small chance of Martin taking pattern by the king who had recognized that some things could not be changed.

A trick of light or shade made the eyes regarding me seem like ebony. 'And I think that turning to the last page is no way to read a book. We're still at the preface. I can promise you equal terms, that's if I'm fool enough to let it happen.' The silky tones made an essentially private conversation into something the world might hear. It was all part of the comic drama we were playing.

'I'm sure, darling, you would never be a fool,' I said as lightly. 'But please elucidate. Let what happen?'

'Let my wife fall in love with someone else,' Martin said smoothly. 'Don't you believe me? You're looking very dubious.'

'As a matter of fact I can't see you in the rôle at all,' I snapped. He would take the double meaning as I intended.

Disconcertingly his eyes flashed. 'What role, then? Tristan? I won't object to that.'

I knew a moment of clear hatred. The evening had made it plain that Clare's right to Chards, to Iceberg and to Martin himself was owned and esteemed. Now, not content with showing me this, he was daring to suggest I had fallen for him. It was insupportable!

Confound it, his eyes were dancing. 'In my book silence gives consent,' he teased. 'Tristan it is.'

It took all I had to maintain control. 'Nothing so romantic. We're not set for a cloak and dagger marriage. And now if you'll excuse me, *I'm* set for bed.' I put my hands to the cane arms of my chair and stood up.

There was a hush of surprise. Clare broke it kindly: 'Of course, Judy. You should have a hot bath – soak those scratches. I'm sure they're sore.'

Martin's hand had gone to the documents on the table. He began unrolling them. It was a strange thing, but I thought his fingers had a fumbling anxious look. 'Before you go, can you take a look at these? I can't hold them over. Clare needs them for a meeting tomorrow.'

'What are they?' I asked suspiciously.

'The plans for Haresmead.' He threw the words away. 'I want to know what you think.'

'You do already.' I was polite but crisp. There were some things one could not feign – surrender over Haresmead was outside the bounds of my contract.

'Yes, but I want to change your mind.' Martin's eyes, I thought crossly, were so clear and unblemished that they gave wrong impressions. At this moment they even looked naïve. 'Five minutes?' he added persuasively.

'I'd rather not,' I said quietly. 'I am – very tired.'

It could be nothing but an attempt to impose his will while others were present. A typical manoeuvre. What a fool I'd be to think he cared!

'In that case there's nothing more to be said.' He let the ends of the roll fly together. 'If you're as sore as all that, get your father to look at you.' He stood up and walked to the door of the verandah. His hands, thrust deep and roughly into his pockets, suggested strain.

'She should,' Clare put in gently. 'They were quite deep cuts. See you, Judy.' She laid her hand affectionately on mine. 'And don't worry.' Her eyes had travelled to Martin's back. Was it possible that she was giving me a message? The generosity touched me.

'If I may say so,' a voice I hardly recognized as Hew's cut sharply into the conversation, 'Judy is due an apology. You don't own her, Martin, she's agreed to marry you and, good grief, that should be enough. If I were in your shoes . . .'

'But you're not.' The words cracked like grape shot. Martin swung round. 'And Judith and I will set ourselves right in time. Let her go, man. She's outgrown the Pony Club.'

Hew's face whitened, and I caught my breath. Martin, brown and firm-chinned, looked at us both for a moment and then strode from the room.

I caught him in the hall. 'That was *unforgivable*!'

'No, Judith,' he said without anger. 'Overdue. And I meant every word.' Not every word, I thought, blazing. Not all that nonsense about him and me setting ourselves right in time.

'Did you see his face?' My voice shook with fury. 'Not that you'd care, of course. You're a juggernaut! Money's your god, that's all you ever think of.'

I had not spoken loudly so the hand that suddenly laid itself against my mouth was insult to injury. So was the force that propelled me into the dining-room.

'Now listen,' Martin said forthrightly, placing his back to the door. 'I did see his face. You had the remedy. You could have looked at my plans. I think you'd have been surprised, certainly you'd have been interested . . .'

'I will never look at them, Martin.' I was calm now and controlled. 'Clare is my brief, remember that. And you don't own me – remember that too.'

'And you, my love?' The twist of the mouth was, if anything, amused. 'Does the cap not fit you as well?'

I hated mockery. I hated an opponent who never lost his temper. I hated the ring on my finger and the responsibilities it imposed. But it said nothing except with my eyes and the flags of hot colour on my cheekbones.

'Then wear it.' His hands went to my shoulders and his mouth to my lips. *Tristan*, I thought, that's the game he's playing. The awful thing was that I could not draw away.

In the end he released me quite gently.

'Judith, why did you dig my garden?' he asked me softly.

'Oh – because I'm a fool,' I answered crossly but honestly.

'You are, you know,' he said caressingly as he opened the door. 'But thank you. Good night.'

CHAPTER SEVEN

It was ironical that the word 'goodnight' was partly responsible for my lying awake. It had been said in such a warm tone.

Martin was so contradictory, ruthless, even cruel, and then suddenly disarming. Why had I dug his garden? I had given the only truthful answer. I didn't know.

The little owls which frequented the woods round St. Keir had stopped hooting by the time I finally dropped off. In consequence it was long past my usual time for rising when I woke. To my astonishment I found Mrs. Trigg in the doorway. She had brought up my breakfast and would not hear of my apologizing for her trouble.

'Not a word, m'dear. All you have to do is eat up and enjoy it.'

The next visitor was my father, ostensibly to check on my wounds, in reality to check on me. He had taken no part in last night's fracas, but that did not mean he was unconcerned.

I knew my refusal to study the plans had disturbed him. I was also well aware that, as he pointed out, I could not shut Irish Iceberg out of my life. When we went back to Dunbeagle the rebuilding would be taking place within a stone's throw of home. In Dad's words there wasn't 'one damn thing I could do'.

'I suppose you are quite sure it tortures you?' he concluded in a deceptively innocent tone. It was one I knew of old. All my childhood agonies had been treated with the same surface gravity. 'You know as well as I do, cobber, we can keep pain alive by refusing to let it go.' He held his hand up as my mouth opened in protest. 'Now, now, now, I'm not saying that at all. Just asking you to have a think about it for Martin's sake.'

Downstairs there was, thank goodness, only Dad in evidence. I had banked on not seeing Martin, who would have left for the factory long ago. Hew's absence was more of a relief than I cared to admit. The thinking process had begun and I was trying to be honest. Much as I cared for Hew, would I ever have married him? Was there much difference between what I had said to him a few nights ago: 'It was such fun when we used to watch the badgers,' and Martin's: 'She's outgrown the Pony Club.'

When I announced that I was going for a walk Dad looked approving. His favourite prescription was fresh air and exercise. Clear the head, he was fond of saying, and you clear the mind.

He even knew the place for me to go. 'If it's peace you're looking for I'll run you into Rock and you can walk over the golf course to St. Enodoc's. It's as good as Dunbeagle, only better.'

Clare had mentioned St. Enodoc's church last night. It was sited amongst sand dunes and on one occasion gale force winds had shifted the sands and buried it. It was reached by a public footpath through the golf course.

Dad put me down where the path began. He did not suggest accompanying me because he guessed my need for solitude. I told him I would find my own way back. Rock was not far from St. Keir and I had a good bump of direction.

'Sure if you get lost you can always send up a flare,' he said comfortably.

'Matches, then,' I requested, stretching out my hand.

'Ah now, don't be so helpless,' I was commanded. 'When I was in the Boy Scouts we used to rub sticks together.'

I looked back after I had gone a few yards and he was still standing on the road beside the car gazing after me. Dad was by way of being a comedian, but today he had not deceived me. I had got him worried and I could have kicked myself.

Preoccupied though I was, the walk was pleasant. The larks were singing and the grassy dips and shoulders of the golf course were starred with yellow charlotte and occasionally the delicate purple of wild orchid. At one place I passed a hollow filled with golden flag irises. And then just as I reached the tiny church with its stumpy broach tower the green land ahead of me dropped and there was the sea.

It had a painted look. Nearly jade arms lay on a breast of sapphire. It could have been the Caribbean, in fact, I was looking towards Daymer Bay and the open Atlantic.

I walked away at last, came to a soft pink hedge of tamarisk and followed my nose into the mini church. There were no visitors besides myself and I looked round it undisturbed, reading the memorials and fascinated by the little line of oil lamps on the vestry shelf. Then I went out again to explore the churchyard.

In Cornwall there is a saint round every corner. All I knew about St. Enodoc came from a booklet on the church table. He had lived in a cave, it said, and had baptized his converts in the Jesus Well down the road. The present church was believed to have been built over the cave. Certainly it had the low thick shape of age.

I picked my steps between the crooked headstones. Some were so old that the lettering was indecipherable, others belonged to my own day. My father had been right. This resting place above the blue cloths of the Camel estuary had peace for the tasting. Each minute scattering clouds peaked up the colour, a lush green slice of bay, a lemon field, and far out the burnished sapphire of the bar.

But gradually I began to feel that I was not the only person enjoying it. I turned slowly and gaped. The figure seated on a bank by the boundary wall got to its feet. It was Martin. Belted jeans and shirt indicated that he was off duty. The shirt was gold brown, open and slim-fitting. I should have been used to Martin's many images, but this one, lithe and golden with a vee of dark fuzz on his chest, was so much my fantasy man on the sherry label that it made me gasp.

'Hello,' he said. 'Welcome to the funk hole.'

'What did you say?' I asked, astonished.

'No desecration intended. I don't doubt St. Enodoc himself used it for that at times. Cornish saints are re-assuringly human. St. Menefreda, for instance, across the way, was one of twenty-four. Her father was St. Brychan who, I think we may say, knew all about it!'

We could say whatever he liked about St. Brychan. It was the funk hole of Martin Trelawney that interested me because, frankly, I couldn't imagine a more redundant fixture. 'You haven't been to work, then?' I remarked.

'It's a matter of opinion. Decision-making isn't my definition of ease. Or tranquillity,' he added as though to himself.

'If I'm interrupting you I'll go.' For once I was not on the attack. I felt almost sympathetic.

'Please don't. You looked as receptive as I am

myself.'

'Yes,' I found myself agreeing. 'Yes, I am. That just expresses it. Dad told me to come here if it was peace I was looking for.'

'I brought your father here. I'm glad,' Martin said quietly. To my relief he made no comment on the remainder of the sentence.

'Summer of a Haughty Man', my one-time title for a portrait of him, recurred. Here we were, it was summer, and as always he looked the part. But Martin was different today. And I was a little different too.

I listened raptly as he unlayered the chapelry's past. Its years of burial under the sands that had piled higher than the eastern gable so that the Vicar of the parish on whom ecclesiastical law laid the duty of an annual visit had been forced to make entry through the roof. The local people who had called it 'sinkininny church'. The great gale of 1857 which had uncovered briefly the traces of a prehistoric forest complete with the horns and teeth of deer. Finally the restoration and the bell bought from a ship which had been wrecked between Daymer Bay and Polzeath.

It was hard to credit such a disaster on today's oiled-silk sea, but there was a natural sand bar at the mouth of the Camel, appropriately christened Doom Bar.

We stood in silence at a headstone in memory of a twenty-year-old lad 'one of the crew of the Peace and Plenty of Lowestoft. Drowned at Trebeterick April 11 1900', and at another with a carved Royal Navy badge and the poignant inscription: 'A seaman of the Great War. S.S. *Armenian*. 28th June 1915. Known Unto God.'

Pain and pleasure seemed to meet somewhere in my throat. I hardly noticed that Martin's hand had slipped into mine.

As we made our way back through the golf course one or two players hailed Martin and he introduced me. It still felt extraordinary to receive good wishes and to hear him being congratulated on our engagement. One lady asked us to drop in for a drink. Her husband inquired how things were going at the works.

'Oh, so-so,' Martin answered. 'We have our problems.

'Tom Grundy?' I asked as we walked on. He looked surprised. 'Was it Tom Grundy you were thinking about in the funk hole?' I amplified.

'Oh, I see. Not directly. I have more important things to consider than Mr. Grundy.' He gave me a sidelong glance. 'He, God willing, will not be a long-term issue.'

'It's Clare, then?' I submitted softly. 'I've been hoping for an opportunity to say how much I liked her.'

'It was mutual,' he acknowledged. 'She's asked me to bring you in tomorrow to see the plant.'

Could I face it? I asked myself sinkingly. Not alone would I feel like a traitor to Dunbeagle, but it would be a certain repetition of yesterday. Iceberg was even more Martin's and Clare's show than Chards.

Martin had given a pleased laugh. 'It's amazing the pride she takes in it. Amazing, that is, for someone who should be getting the kids off to school. No, I don't mean she has kids, just that at heart she's a perfect unliberated woman.'

'Surely a very male chauvinistic remark,' I put in. 'Which speaking personally I would resent and resist.'

'Speaking of you,' he grinned. 'I would know better.'

I had had my answer. Perhaps I should have left it there. 'I don't really see much difference between Clare and myself. She's obviously super at her job.'

'That's been said. But it's a miracle. Clare like you? No more than chalk is like cheese.'

The mood was lighthearted, but I could not help feeling that every word was meant.

'If you could have seen yourselves last night,' he went on, 'you wouldn't need me to tell you.'

It was easy enough to see Clare, thick brown hair turning under, face with contours that would round nicely after a holiday, knee-length dress stunning but simple. 'At heart a perfect unliberated woman.' (Whose heart? I did not need to ask.) In other words a woman a man could cherish.

And myself? Lay me in the sun for months and I would never round. I had a Saluki frame and straight hair. What had I been wearing last night? A long skirt, air force blue, falling from a gathered waistband. Two big

97

patch pockets with cuffs. A long-sleeved blouse flowered in grey and brown.

'Oh well,' I said defensively. 'I had to cover up my scratches.'

'Covered or uncovered, you're much more sophisticated than Clare. Dammit, girl, you may be a failed artist, but you have got yourself half-way round the world.'

This was too much. 'Who says I'm a failed artist?' I demanded hotly.

'Who has ever seen proof that you aren't?' he cornered.

'Are you buying?' I asked crisply.

'Our design team is always on the lookout for new talent. Why not talk to them tomorrow? But don't be disappointed if nothing comes of it. Standards are high these days, they have to be. Printing firms no longer have their own designers, so when we send them patterns each design must be perfect. And naturally it must be commercial. If it's for the export market then it must appeal in the country it's going to. If it's for the home market a different selling point may be needed. In other words, it's not enough to draw a pretty picture.'

'I would never have guessed,' I said sarcastically. 'But you explain it so beautifully.'

The unexpected happened. He clipped me smartly on the seat of my pants.

It changed the atmosphere. We laughed at a golden labrador sitting bored but patient as his mistress putted. I remarked a wild orchid and Martin said Clare loved them and he would try and find a few for her. He had a nice little handful, I just three blooms, when one of the golfers bore down on me and reproached me for picking them. 'They take seven years to grow again,' she explained.

I had had no idea, and I was abashed. Martin with far greater soils had had the presence of mind to hide them behind his back. He chuckled heartlessly and reminded me that in some respects it was still a man's world.

'I suggest we make this an occasion of equal rights,' he added, and handed me half the posy.

'You're too kind, sir,' I told him, taking it.

They were lovely little flowers, all the more so if, as my informant had said, they took seven years to blossom. I kept looking at them as Martin drove home.

Seven years ago I had just met Martin. Until then I had been very young. Christmas seven years ago I had started to grow up. And at the same time deep and dark in the Cornish winter the seed of a wild orchid had begun its journey to flower.

We had the same span and we would both be plucked and left to wither.

Sentimental twaddle, I thought crossly, what was I thinking of?

Whatever decision Martin had come to in the funk hole, he seemed cheerful. As the car sped towards home and Mrs. Trigg's good lunch he began to whistle. It was the tune I'd heard him lilt in the little inn, though then he had put the words to it.

It had been a song about love, love and the picking of flowers.

At breakfast next morning Hew proposed that we take a picnic lunch and drive first to Tintagel and then on to the moor. He looked at me sharply when I explained that Martin was taking me to see the factory. Why not leave that for a wet day? he suggested. This one was perfect for Bodmin. We would probably see fox cubs – he had watched a trio at play there last week.

It was tempting, but I had made up my mind. Hew's face darkened. 'You've changed,' he said reproachfully. 'You used to enjoy my company.'

'And still do, but I'm engaged now,' I pointed out.

'Here we go again,' he muttered. 'What are you afraid of? No, don't answer that. It's a six-letter word beginning with M. Judy, what is this madness? If you were happy I wouldn't press it, but you're not.'

The words echoed tauntingly as I slipped into the car. A word of welcome from Martin would not have come amiss, but he had more important things on his mind. Two union officials were coming to see him that day. In consequence he would be unable to conduct my tour in person.

'However, Clare will be there and I've arranged for Peter Harcourt to join you for lunch. Peter is our chief designer. I'm sure you'll find what he has to say of interest and value.'

The car headed for Wadebridge at a speed which made it a near thing for a little stoat running across the road.

I asked if the meeting with the union men meant trouble.

'I hope it means avoiding it,' Martin answered. Negotiations on a pay claim were in train. He had every hope that progress was being made. 'It's a lovely day,' he added. 'I'm not sure you shouldn't have waited till it rained.'

You could not say that the red carpet was being put out for me. Hew had been right, I owned silently. This farce was madness. It would achieve nothing.

The Iceberg plant was between Bugle and St. Austell. After Wadebridge we went south into the china clay region. Prepared as I was for it, the landscape of white pyramids was astonishing.

China clay is Cornwall's finest industry and we were driving through the heart of it. Where sites were in production there were swinging cranes, climbing trolley buckets and lorries. But far and away the greatest impression was fantasy. Martin had promised me 'the mountains of the moon' and here they were, peak after peak, ghost-white, strange and silent as space.

Martin explained that china clay was a form of moist granite which, when purified, was identical with Chinese kaolin or porcelain clay. It was used in varying proportions for the manufacture of earthenware, bone china and porcelain, and not unexpectedly it gave whiteness to the mix. His clear and concise descriptions of how it was excavated, separated and refined were a proof of how well he knew his stuff.

My thinking may have been a bit muddled, but I felt it was the Cornishman in him that spoke. Cornishmen, he had once told me, were brought up to clay and to tin and to the sea.

I could have listened for ever, but all too soon we left

the white spoil heaps and the green pit pools and reached a busy crossroads. Minutes later came a spread of factory buildings and signboard THE ICEBERG GROUP.

We drove through the yard to a parking space marked 'Managing Director'. The buildings overlooking us varied. The giant warehouses and the laboratory were modern, the main factory, brick-walled and gaunt, was probably a centenarian. On the other hand, the administration block into which Martin conducted me was play group age. A plaque gave its official opening as 1974.

There was something Finnish about the public area, pale pinewood, small ceramic tiles and a wall tapestry boldly yellow and terracotta.

Martin's office was more conventional. There was a lot of beautiful red mahogany. Skirting boards and a long built-in storage unit glowed against the oyster wallpaper. I remarked an intriguing sculpture, a black bull wearing a garland.

'No china shop should be without one,' Martin said dryly.

Iceberg, I noted, took care of the gaffer. A selection of the day's papers awaited him on a side table and hard on our heels came a waitress with a tray.

'Ah, Doris, just the job,' Martin greeted her appreciatively.

The tray's contents were as good-looking as the rest of the room, the coffee set stainless steel, the cups and saucers orange bone china.

'Didn't he do well?' I commented mischievously.

He looked at me over the coffee pot which he was holding. 'What? This? If you want to know, the extent of my interest is about one spoon.'

'Not even the bull?'

'Oh yes, I own him. He was given to me in Greece. Someone thought he looked like me.'

It needed no skill to deduce that the someone was female. More pertinent and strangely warming was the frankness on his assets.

'The rest is image,' Martin added. '*Pro bono publico.* My needs are simple. A place must be safe, sound and clean.' I wondered why I should find it so disarming. Or

101

why it should make me think back, seven years plus, to the lad who had cleared out Hew's cottage and earned no thanks for it. 'I should tell you—' Martin's voice died. 'Come in,' he called instead. 'Ah, Clare, just in time for coffee.'

Clare had had her sights trained on the parking lot for Martin's car to come in. The union officials had arrived early, someone called Gerald was holding the fort for the moment.

It meant that coffee dalliance was over. 'You'll look after Judith, then,' Martin said briefly. 'If I can, I'll join you for lunch.'

'Some hopes,' Clare prophesied as the door closed. 'You'll be lucky if he has the last waltz with you.'

'Is he always as busy as this?' I asked diffidently.

There was a little pause. Clare must have been a very pretty child and this morning she was looking charming in stripes and spring green. The spring green was a collarless suit with a pleated skirt, the stripes a toning silk blouse. Her colour rose slightly as she studied me. 'It's the way to his heart, Judy. Take the word of an expert.'

Plainly she was recalling my refusal to look at the plans for Haresmead.

I found it pretty devastating. You silly, incredible person, Clare Weston, I thought angrily, we're rivals. Don't act like Sir Galahad.

Besides, I was ruffled. Martin was not all tycoon, he sat cuddly kangaroos to the breakfast table, he played poker with funny friendly old men and he sat in churchyards thinking out what to do. *Was* Clare such an expert? Undoubtedly she was. I was the novice who had made such a bad showing.

Next minute I was laughing at the absurdity. I had actually started to worry about my inadequacies, about hurting Clare and about the insuperable effort Iceberg would demand of me.

And, of course, none of it was for real.

I'm laughing, I told myself. It didn't feel much like it.

'Shall we make a move – if you're ready?' Clare suggested politely. 'There's a lot to see.'

She was right. We started off with the clays themselves and we ended up back in Administration in the display area. Much had happened in between. The mix (Cornish Iceberg made earthenware and bone china and there was a different formula for each) had gone to the moulds and then to the kilns. The biscuit firing over, the pieces had been decorated, glazed and fired again at a lower temperature.

Our journey had not, of course, taken as long as the transformation of a measure of clay into a gleaming article displayed on a sage green or kingfisher drape, but the works were vast and my questions had been far-reaching. It was almost lunchtime when we finally fetched up in the display hall. This, in its own right, was a room of grace and beauty. Yorkshire Iceberg were glass cutters and had supplied chandeliers that blazed as brightly as any Viennese ballroom.

Today they had something to blaze about. The array of finished goods was entrancing. Bright earthenwares ranged from art nouveau flowers to a heavy pattern of baskets and cornflowers. Pansies crowded the rim of a cream plate. Hollyhocks swarmed a cylindrical coffee pot. There was a charming tea-set with turquoise saucers and decorated cups and plates. An ochre breakfast set had metallic bases and shiny insides.

The more elegant bone china was beautiful. Sprigged cups and saucers, very white with thin gilding. A tea-set called Red Ribbon from a Swiss design. A fluted green gravy boat with a lilac spray decoration. Leaf dishes patterned in butterflies and, amongst the moderns, a range called Larkfield with a wild flower design in royal blue and aqua.

When we went to the dining-room I suspected that the executives who normally used it had been whittled down on my account. There were only four place settings at the polished table. Peter Harcourt, chief designer, was waiting as arranged and took us into an anteroom for drinks.

While we were having these, Martin's head came round the door. It explained the fourth place at the table.

'Well, darling, have we passed?' he asked so naturally that as always I had to remind myself that I was not his darling and my opinion of Iceberg could not have mattered less.

'Have you talked to Peter as I suggested?' Martin pursued. He nodded understandingly when I explained that we had only just arrived. 'Fine. You won't need us, then. I want Clare, I'm afraid.' The union meeting had adjourned until three and Martin thought she should sit in on the next session. There were also several points on which he wanted her views in private.

'Sorry to do this to you,' he apologized. 'But we must talk. We'll get something in the Duke of York.' It was a pub I had noticed on the way in.

I stopped myself from thinking 'How convenient.' Martin and Clare met business crises every day. If lunch *à deux* sounded intimate the chances were they would discuss only the union negotiations. And yet ... they could be talking about me. He could be giving her the chance to show that our engagement had disturbed her. He would have to do this, I argued, it was part of the bargain.

'I'll tell you what, Peter, this looks like a late job,' Martin concluded. 'When you've had your chat with Judith perhaps you'd organize her transport. All right, darling?' He turned to me. 'See you tonight – if you're still up!'

Would he kiss me? I was half expecting it, but he contented himself with a smile. The attention centred on Clare, who had not finished her drink. She looked very young as he finally hustled her out.

It was absurd to feel deflated, especially as Peter Harcourt was such a nice person. I could not have hoped for a more sympathetic listener as I told him where I had been and the different studies I had undertaken.

'I must sound like the perpetual student!' I ended.

Peter assured me that there was no need to feel shame or discouragement. Had I not told him that a shop in Sydney had exhibited my paintings and that most of them had been sold? And had I not also said that a publishing firm in London had taken some sketches for their book jackets? 'Perhaps you've been too much artist and not enough artisan. A designer must recognize practicalities. Let me explain.'

He did so with pains and patience. Tableware must have a happy relationship with food. Hectic colours might not appeal to the palate, trendy motifs soon lost their appeal to the eye. Iceberg demanded that a decoration be well drawn, well coloured and well placed. Here he went into serviceability and the different glazing processes. They were all things to bear in mind.

The works were at present researching a new type of stoneware which would be flameproof. If the tests were successful and the product marketed the group would be breaking new ground and the range would receive maximum publicity. It offered a wide field to any aspiring decorator. The prospect was exciting.

Peter had been talking quickly and name-dropping. Suddenly he paused. 'Look, am I confusing you? Can you distinguish period? This design, for instance.' He took a side plate off the table and handed it to me. 'Iceberg 1974. What is it from?'

The table had been charmingly set with deep blue place mats. The candles in the silver centrepiece matched them exactly. The china had an elaborate border with figures that could have been dragons or griffons. If the latter, the design was French rather than Oriental. The colour decided me, it was a beautiful rich turquoise.

'Oriental pattern,' I said firmly. 'Chinese. I'd put the original as middle Ming.'

'Well done,' Peter commended. 'Ten out of ten. Now have you anything you can show me?'

He had said enough to fire me, but I had to explain my present lack of materials. It was soon rectified by a loan from the studio.

There was still no sign of the meeting breaking up, so Peter sent me home in one of the firm's cars. When I thanked him for the help he had given me he assured me that it had been a pleasure and added that, although the engagement had not yet been announced, he hoped he might offer his good wishes and those of all the design team.

'I daresay you felt the eyes on you as you went through. Clare told me they goggled! And I don't blame them. He must be lousy at cards!'

I doubted if cards had ever featured much in Martin's busy life. Certainly he had not been the star of the hospital poker school. But it had not brought him the time-honoured consolation. He was not lucky in love. If eventually he won Clare it would be through skill and hard work – and me.

Suddenly it was a burdensome thought.

CHAPTER EIGHT

I SPENT the evening with my sketching block. The intertwining circles and arabesques were quite pleasing now that I could colour them. The design was obviously one for earthenware.

I also made some sketches for china, the first a sort of memory test for myself to see how far I could recapture the classical French decoration in the spirit of Sèvres, the second a much lighter style with a wild orchid motif. This pas partly an exercise in placing. I put a single large flower at the bottom of the cup and made the wide border a multitude of tiny blossoms.

'In the name of goodness, what's going on out here?' my father demanded, coming to the door of the sun porch where I was working. It was past eleven and he was on his way to bed.

I had not noticed the hour. It was a shock in more ways than one. Could Martin's meeting have lasted all this time?

'May I see?' Hew inquired, joining us.

It was ridiculous to feel shy, but things had changed between us. Now he examined the drawing in silence. I needed no explanation of his feelings; he was thinking, quite rightly, that I had turned my coat.

'Is this what you're going in for in future?' he asked at length.

'It depends what people think of it.' I tried to be lighthearted.

'People will think it couldn't be more Iceberg,' he said cruelly. 'Martin is certainly getting good value for his money.'

'You couldn't be more wrong!' The words burst forth unchecked.

'Oh?' Hew's brow had furrowed.

It was a warning. 'Martin is not marrying me to get a designer on the cheap,' I said carefully. 'If you must know, he's marrying me for love.'

It was so very nearly true that my conscience made no fuss. Martin *had* asked me to marry him for love – even if it was for love of Clare.

'And the sooner the better!' The voice made me jump. Martin must have put the car in the garage and walked across the grass. He closed the door while I stood fascinated by the timing. Next instant his arm had gone lovingly round my shoulders. 'Knows her lines, doesn't she?' he said laughingly. 'I don't think she'll be any trouble.'

'I'm afraid she took me too literally.' Hew was also laughing. He patted my hand. 'Judy, don't you know envy when you see it? I didn't mean they were going to hog your designs. I just meant that when you walked through the plant with him today he must have been the proudest guy in Cornwall.'

There was a sharp silence. The contrast between the supposition and the reality seemed to catch me by the throat.

Martin was the first to speak. 'If she's word-perfect you're not,' he told Hew. 'I had this union negotiator all day. I'm not sure who showed Judith round, but regrettably I didn't.'

'Well, I'll be damned!' Hew shook his head in amazement. 'No wonder she's edgy. You'd better do something about it. Tomorrow is Saturday.'

'It's perfectly all right,' I said firmly. 'I don't need pampering.' Martin must not take me out from a sense of duty, or because he had been told to. I knew Hew meant to be kind, but I would find it intolerable.

'But of course you do, he's absolutely right,' Martin

assured me smoothly. 'Though I never pamper women — as you'll find out in time.'

He did not ask to look at the sketches and I put them away and went thankfully to bed.

The matter should have ended there, but to my embarrassment I heard Martin inform Mrs. Trigg next morning that he and I would be out for lunch. It was the day Hew had arranged to play golf with Clare and he invited Dad to join them. My father, however, was more than happy with his own company.

'Well, we're certainly not falling for that one!' Hew stated lightly. 'If you don't want to play gooseberry, Jack, which I can understand, there'll be no danger with Clare and me.'

Dad, however, stuck to his guns and the arrangement was agreed. Not too easily, though. Hew argued vehemently before accepting defeat. I concluded that, old friend as she was, he did not want to be alone with Clare. He knew how things stood between her and Martin and did not wish to take sides on the engagement issue. It was completely in character.

When I went to make my own plea for independence it was turned down.

'Do I have to remind you of the contract?' Martin was rubbing the windscreen and did not so much as look up.

'Not at every turn you don't,' I said shortly. 'I'm tired of feeling like a cow at a fair.'

'Heifer,' he amended laconically. 'At least so I assume.'

This I ignored. 'You don't mind Hew and Clare spending the day together?'

'Not in the least. Do you think I should?' He gave the rear window a polish and tossed the duster into the car.

'I thought he seemed embarrassed.'

'Maybe. He'll get over it.' Martin opened the door. '*You* look lovely.'

'You haven't even looked at me,' I retorted, and could have bitten my tongue out.

'I have you in my mind's eye — continually. "A daughter of the gods, divinely tall and most divinely fair." ' He was facing me now.

'That's enough nonsense,' I said hastily, and slid into the seat.

Martin's way of telling me that we were going to Padstow on the opposite point of the estuary was enigmatic. 'Why don't we talk about unpampered women? Have you ever walked the plank?' He added a casual apology for the previous day. 'Sorry you had to go home alone. It couldn't be helped.'

I asked him how the meeting had ended.

'At ten o'clock with a lot of sore heads. But they're putting the proposals to a mass meeting on Tuesday and recommending acceptance. Actually it was a good discussion – fair-mindedness all round. And Clare is a tremendous help on these occasions. They like her and she never loses her cool.'

We parked the car at Rock and went out over the white sand to a waiting motor launch. There was a plank to run over and an iron ladder to climb. Then it was all aboard and we were threading the silting golden sands that were fast depriving Padstow of its shipping.

I sat gazing. The headlands like sleeping green lizards stretched out between sky and sea. One school of thought held that when Tristan had brought Isolde to Cornwall their ship had sailed up the Camel estuary. I wondered if it had been a summer day like this one. I wondered how it felt to be bound against all reason to a man one should hate and to know one would never escape him. I wondered if Isolde had had any hope that one day her story would end happily.

'Penny for them,' Martin teased.

'They're rejects,' I said firmly.

'Perhaps not,' he answered unexpectedly. 'Perhaps I can even do something about it.'

'Nothing would surprise me more,' I retorted truthfully. 'But what did you have in mind?'

'That fate has dropped you into an enchanted patch with the wrong man.' Regardless of the other passengers he put his hand under my chin and turned my face expertly towards his own. 'You're missing the Pony Club, aren't you?'

'Martin, please,' I whispered embarrassedly. 'Not here. I'm okay.'

'You're not, Judy, you're unhappy.' At least he had dropped his voice. 'If it's not Hew I'm stumped.'

He had said it for me. I could not fathom myself. Things were taking their predictable course, Martin was giving Clare food for thought and me a good time. There was every reason for satisfaction and none for the miseries. But miseries I had, hard as I tried to hide them.

As I looked at them the dark eyes softened.

'We'll have exactly the day he'd have given you,' Martin said gently. 'Trust me. You'll enjoy it, I promise.' He added a question: 'Have you ever been picked up?'

'Now and then,' I said guardedly.

'This is now,' he informed me. 'Take hand, lady. Come ashore. Me magic man. You have good day, much to laugh about.'

The words were to echo not once but many times; the day I was to remember all my life. Its moments whirled away in a storm of happiness.

Low tide prevented the ferry entering harbour. We clambered like children over the rocks and walked down a field path. Today the grass was high and the sun was shining, but one could imagine dark nights when lanterns had bobbed along the cliff and stealthy figures went to meet a boat.

Martin's shirt was copper red, his throat and the backs of his hands were ground in brown. I can't explain it, but he seemed to carry me along with him as he sang:

"So you will pick the lilies and I'll pick the thyme."

'Thyme or time?' I asked him.

His eyes answered me wickedly.

Padstow was old and very Cornish and I loved it on sight. It was built round the harbour and scattered white with seagulls. We watched a fisherman making a net with orange cord, chose picture postcards from the revolving stands, drank coffee out of pink cups, ate thick squares of shortbread and looked in the seashell shop.

Martin bought me a doll dressed as a smuggler with a

patch over one eye and I bought him a green piskie to sit on his desk. We found a window display of Capodimonte figures and a wonderful book shop and when Martin couldn't prise me away from a book on pottery he purchased it and stuck it under my arm.

I had seen the price and I was alarmed. 'No, Martin. It's very dear.'

'So are you!' he rejoined lightly. 'What was it he used to call you? I know it was something extraordinary. Judy, me old sagacious?'

The word brought me down to earth. You forgot, I accused myself roughly, he's trying to make you happy. He told you today he's Hew.

Aloud I made a laugh of it: 'Respect, please. The word is "segocia". It's Dublin for "darling".'

He had cheated. He had got so close to me that we had finished each other's sentences and our feet had known instinctively when to halt. It had been an unconscious ballet. I knew it sounded mad, I could describe it no better.

Never, never, never had I felt like this with Hew.

Suddenly I had to make conversation. Martin had been singing that song again, but only those same few lines.

'Is that all there is or all you know?'

'Ah!' he said teasingly. He sang it and I listened – and thought I got the message.

> ' "For lilies they do wither,
> Thyme will come soon
> And the red rose it will blossom
> All in the month of June." '

It was obvious Clare had given him grounds for hope.

We bought our lunch, hot Cornish pasties, green grapes and a couple of cans of beer and picnicked on a seat above the harbour. The ropes round the bollards were Cornish blue and the seagulls mustered on the slipway and screamed at us for scraps. I opened my beautiful book and read about eastern pots, blue colouring and the Great Silk Road from Samarkand to China. Martin moved nearer and we read it together, his arm round my shoulder.

All at once I had an inspiration for Peter's new flame-proof ware. Casseroles and egg coddlers scattered with seashells. In minutes we had crossed the square to the shell shop. It had been fascinating enough on the first visit, now it was treasure trove.

As I looked the pattern rose before me, curly white conches, little cowries, rose murex, amber and pink cameos, purply brown gourdlike sea-urchins. I was so excited that I could not wait. Martin bought me a sketching pad and we found a seat and put our heads together. I worked like lightning – time enough for polishing when I got home. Placing was important, but the colours would be no problem, nature's own scheme was unbeatable. I saw it as a symphony shading from pink to rose, cream to amber, amethyst to brown, white to palest grey.

We even thought of a name for it, Trevose, after the headland.

'I think it's good,' I said tremulously.

'I know it is,' Martin returned. 'May we have it? Subject to our paying your price.'

'That's all right,' I told him. 'Mr. Magic Man picked up the bill.'

Despite the squawking of the seagulls it seemed very quiet. Martin's cheek was close to mine. 'You're a sweet and generous person. I warned you once you had a run-away heart.'

I knew he was going to kiss me and I knew I wanted him to.

'It's a nice way of doing business,' he said lightly as his lips left mine. It was as good as saying to me, 'Get involved at your peril.'

Soon afterwards the ferry boat came in flying the Red Ensign and with pink fenders bobbing against her sides. There might be thirty minutes or so before we reached home, but to all intents and purposes the day was over.

The engine chugged and we pulled away over water that was now peacock blue against the fringes of white sand. Again I looked at the cliffs so green and innocent in the sunshine. You might be hard put to it to run a boat in through the dark on dangerous sands, my contraband came by lips and eyes and in a snatch of folk song. Fool that I was, I was smuggling an invisible import.

It was crazy, incredible, impossible – I'd kept my eyes open for seven years – but it had happened.

I'd fallen in love at last, and my love did not love me.

'What shall we do tomorrow?' Martin asked as we ran up the sands at Rock to where we had left the car. He made several suggestions, all of which sounded delightful, but by now I had myself in check.

'If you want to work, please don't think I have to be entertained.'

'I thought we'd agreed that lilies wither,' Martin returned.

It seemed an unkind way of reminding me that this was strictly short-term. Besides, I associated lilies with death.

'Perhaps they'd last longer unpicked,' I said shortly.

'Undoubtedly,' he agreed. 'But what a waste!'

Dad too seemed to have enjoyed his day. Hew was less communicative. He had gone back to Clare's house for dinner and it was late when he came in looking thoughtful if not burdened. I hated to surmise that my idyllic day had been the cause of unhappiness but, also, it seemed so.

The weather forecast had been poor, but next morning when I woke the sun was shining brightly and my father was in the garden casting a professional eye on Martin's roses. They had had a discussion the previous night about their needing iron. I dressed and went out to join him.

It was still an hour to breakfast time and Dad suggested a walk. We went past woods where a few evenings ago at dusk a little owl had mewed at me and I had thought it a cat. Since yesterday I had been toying with the idea of a set of bird designs, the shop in Padstow had had some beautiful bird-patterned porcelain beside the Capodimonte. Now my thoughts centred excitingly on owls.

'We'd better step on it – look at the sky,' Dad remarked as we neared the home stretch. Dark clouds were already scudding across the sun.

Big drops spattered the road as we got within sight of Chards. At the same moment a car backed out of the garage by the Jack and Jill wall and shot away up the road.

'Was that Martin?' Dad asked. 'Or was it Hew?'

Both cars were the same colour, but Hew's was a smaller model and he seldom bothered to garage it.

'Martin,' I said flatly.

'Perhaps he's just gone to get a paper,' Dad opined.

Something told me differently. I was not in the least surprised when Hew met us in the hall. 'You didn't see Martin? He left his apologies.'

Hew, it seemed, did not want to look at me. When Dad asked: 'What for?' he looked uncomfortable, the way Hew always looked when he had to give bad news.

'He doesn't know when he'll be back,' he said diffidently. 'Clare rang. She wanted him urgently.'

The morning was memorable for two things – the weather and Hew's kindness. The storm broke while we were having breakfast. Vivid lightning forked across the garden and Mrs. Trigg who was scared of thunder worried about the big elm tree at the side of the house.

When the worst of the storm had passed Hew looked at his watch and suggested church. I was sure he sensed that left to myself I would have passed a miserable morning. Hew always did know that sort of thing. Visits to the dentist, disappointing exam results, in fact anything which gave me the blues, he had always been able to prescribe for.

I could never quite get used to the new Hew, especially this morning in a smart blue suit and carrying an umbrella. The umbrella was for me since the car could not go right to the church door. When we got out, Hew gave me his arm and we ran. 'Like old times,' he said smilingly.

The church, noted for its wood carvings, was beautiful. Service over, Hew took me round it, pointing out the pew ends. The vicar shook hands with us and Hew introduced me as an old friend.

Outside, the rain had eased and we looked at some picturesque cottages.

'They say it's an ill wind,' Hew observed humorously.

'Do you know why Clare wanted Martin?' I asked as we drove home.

'Haven't an earthly. It happens so often I don't ask any more. It's not always domestic, of course. Sometimes it's Iceberg, but today being Sunday I must confess I didn't think of that. The last time she rang on a Sunday her cat was stuck somewhere.'

'Oh,' I said indifferently.

So it was always happening, was it? If I were wise I would remember that.

Some time later Mrs. Trigg announced that Mrs. Weston was on the telephone and wanting to speak to me.

'Judy? I wondered.' Clare's voice had a puzzled ring. 'I've just been on to Martin and you didn't seem to be there. Look, I know it's a bore, but company means a great deal at a time like this. Could you get Hew or someone to drive you over?' Her previous call to Martin had been an 'early warning'. Tom Grundy, a familiar name, was again stirring up trouble. There had been noises about an unofficial strike or a sit-in, and Martin had gone over. Clare felt she should have been with him, but she'd had a long-standing arrangement to visit her sister in hospital which he would not hear of her cancelling.

'I didn't know anything about it,' I began defensively. Clare's tone was annoyingly proprietorial. 'As a matter of fact no one knew where he'd gone.'

'Oh.' The hesitation was only momentary. 'Well, let's not waste time on that,' Clare continued. 'You know now. Hew will drive you, I'm sure, if you ask him.'

'Just a minute, Clare.' My head was whirling. 'Are you sure Martin would want me?'

'What do you think?' she chuckled, and rang off.

Mostly what I thought at that moment was that Clare Weston was an amazing woman. I had known she was strong, but this seemed superhuman. *Unless she did not care for Martin.*

I was horrified at my sudden shaft of hope. It was wild, crazy and futile. Nothing had changed, nothing, *nothing.* Even if Clare were heartwhole Martin still loved her. It could be embarrassing if I turned up at the factory unasked.

On the other hand Clare would make it her business to discover whether or not I had done so, and if I had not she might think me an odd kind of fiancée.

The ring on my finger added its quota as a devil's advocate. 'Act worthily,' it reminded.

It's different now, now that I know I'm going to get hurt, I thought childishly.

But of course it was not different. Anyone who had ever tried to live by a rule had got hurt.

'Oh, lord!' I said aloud, and went in search of Hew.

'I must say it's not my idea of how to spend Sunday,' he observed as we drove.

'It is an emergency,' I countered.

'Yes, I know. Routine where Martin is concerned. He'll be committing bigamy, you know, love. He's married already – to Iceberg.'

Dangerous ground. 'I'll cross that bridge when I come to it.'

'Well, it's your bridge,' Hew said resignedly. 'I can't stop you. I can only say that I love you and I know the way to make you happy. There's just one thing, Judy.' He had coloured. 'There's been a change in my affairs. I'm in a better position . . .'

'To keep me in the style to which I've been accustomed,' I chipped in, glad of the diversion.

'Something like that.'

It was touching. 'Oh, my dear, dear Hew,' I said tremulously, 'as if that mattered! I couldn't rate you any higher if you owned O.P.E.C.'

He put me down at the factory gate, sketched a wave and drove off. I hated myself as I went across the yard. He was always so willing to help, so kind and so loving. He would give me, if needs be, the coat off his back and he would keep me safe. But all I felt was sadness, a sort of autumn sadness.

It was answer enough.

The factory appeared to be working or at least to have some of its work force in. There were cars and motorbikes on the parking lot and the doors were open. I was glad of that as I made my way inside. No one challenged me, but in blue jeans and a blazer I attracted no attention. Several employees were similarly dressed.

It was very different from Friday when the administration block had been humming with activity. Today it had an eerie stillness. Martin's door was open and I put my head round it.

Martin was at the window, his foot up on one of the elegant chairs. He was whittling a piece of wood. A patterned shirt of navy blue cotton and belted fawn check trousers emphasized his slim build. He looked a mere boy.

And he was astonished. 'Good grief, *Judith*!' Whatever it was he was carving went hurriedly out of sight.

I felt awkward. 'Clare thought I should come. She phoned.'

His face was expressionless. 'She's in Plymouth seeing her sister. She worries more than she need. I don't know what she told you.' He came forward, closed the door and ushered me to a chair. 'I wouldn't have asked you, I'm sure you know that.'

It was becoming plainer every minute that I was superfluous, if not in the way. 'In the circumstances I felt I should come. I didn't want to give her the impression that there was anything artificial about the engagement.'

'Quite so. Clare is such a bore about marriage. She sees it as togetherness.'

'Shouldn't she?' Too late I saw the twinkle in the dark eyes. 'You're making fun of me,' I said crossly.

'You are so anxious, my love, to underline your position. I know you didn't come of your own volition, but I never look a gift horse in its beautiful mouth. Truthfully, you're welcome.'

'Truthfully I'd nothing better to do.' Push me hard enough and I could be generous too. 'And it was an opportunity to bring these for Peter Harcourt. He asked for a sample of my work.'

I put the folder of designs on the desk, wondering why showing them to Martin should make me feel so peculiar. He studied all of them intently – the blue and green wavy curves, the ornate French-inspired arabesque heavy in gold and dark blue, the wild orchid motif delicately starred and the shells. The shells were my favourite and not only because of sentiment. I felt they had originality and the colours had come up well.

At all cost I had to be cool.

'These are very good,' Martin said at last. He put the shells and the wild orchids in the centre of the desk and gazed at them. 'It strikes me you're not only a gift horse but a dark one as well. I have been teaching my grand-mother to suck eggs.'

'Your grandmother is duly complimented,' I told him.

'They might need some modification to suit colouring or glazing.' He tapped the shells. 'Obviously we would want to preserve this intact, it's beautiful. I'm not sure if it would run us into extra firing. However, these are tech-nicalities. I'll have Peter look at them tomorrow.'

As he put the sketches back in the folder I asked him what had been happening.

'A few hotheads with a kangaroo court mentality' were spoiling for a fight. There were legitimate claims, as I knew negotiations were in progress and voting would take place on Tuesday. Tom Grundy and his supporters had dredged up a number of trumpery matters which had not got union backing and were trying to take over.

The works were on special overtime for a big American order. All but a handful had walked out of the afternoon shift and were meeting at this moment in the recreation hall. The shop stewards had been trying to get them back, but there was still no telling how things would go.

'What have you been doing?' I asked curiously.

'Waiting,' he said simply. 'With the door open. Man-agement doors are open all over industry today. There are those who call it a gimmick. It was never that here in my uncle's day, he pioneered it long before it became procedure.'

'I know very little about Iceberg,' I began.

'And show as little desire to learn.' He had a smiling way of hitting you. 'If your attitude to the Isolde plans is anything to go by.'

'That is still rape,' I said stormily.

'So was this, I suppose, one day. Westminster Abbey

118

probably blocked someone's view of the river.' He played with the knife he had been using. 'We make beautiful things, Judith, your Trevose pattern for instance will delight wherever it goes. Does that not give us some right to exist?'

It was an important question and one which had not escaped me.

'In reason, of course, it must,' I answered honestly. 'Emotionally no. I could never care about a factory.'

'And yet you're here. Waiting with me to see which way they'll go when they come out of the meeting, right into the plant for what's left of the shift or straight ahead through the gates and home. We may still have to wait for hours, I can't get you anything to eat because the canteen is closed. You could be at home with Hew and your father, but you're here. I wonder why?'

'I told you why, Martin. In case Clare might get the wrong idea.'

'Ah yes, of course, Clare. I almost forgot,' he said softly.

It was a strange afternoon; the thunder was still circling, there were heavy showers and the air was humid and desperately oppressive. 'Fighting weather,' Martin said once. 'We need a wind of change.'

He lit a cigarette and suddenly started talking. Iceberg had three plants in England, each specialists in their particular field. The St. Austell works had begun life as Trelawney & Sons but had joined the big group ten years ago. The Trelawney running it at the time had been Martin's uncle, he who had instituted the rule of the open door.

His name had been John and he had seen Trelawneys through the war years and their difficult aftermath. It was somehow a shock to learn that Hew was John Trelawney's only son.

Martin had much less to say about his own father, Rick, brother of John but by tacit admission quite unlike him. Rick Trelawney, as Hew had told me in the past, had gone to live in America when his marriage failed.

A lot of threads were now forming a pattern in my mind, but the most interesting ones had yet to come.

They concerned Martin himself, his home life and how at the age of thirty he came to be in control.

'My uncle died some years ago,' he said briefly. 'It was always my ambition to succeed him and they backed me. That's about it.'

'They?' I echoed.

'The bank when they bailed us out.' He broke off to glance at the door. 'Come in, gentlemen. Are we ready to talk?'

The three men who entered looked understandably surprised at finding me in the room. Martin made the necessary introductions and then put the car keys into my hand. 'Go ahead, darling. I'll make my own way.'

As I went out one of the shop stewards was saying: 'Do you want a lift, Mr. Trelawney?'

I hoped the cordial tone was a good omen. Good or bad, however, I had no intention of leaving without Martin. If it was a waiting game I would play it till the last second of injury time.

That was what it had suddenly become, a gripping cliff-hanging game. In the car my eyes stayed riveted to the door of the recreation hall. It was all-important that the stream of people when it did emerge should turn to the right.

I was impatient, grudging the minutes, wishing I could be a fly on the wall of Martin's office.

It seemed a long time. Rain washed the windscreen and bounced off the roofs of the parked cars. At last someone came to the door of the recreation hall. She put her hand out and squealed: 'It's lashing!' Others joined her in the doorway. They too exclaimed at the rain, then they put their heads down and ran.

I sat holding my breath as one by one the runners, both male and female, veered right across the loading bay and in through the factory door. The last man stopped to stub out his cigarette.

As he too vanished into the hallway Martin came out of the administration block. I waved excitedly and he came over. I saw his lips framing the words: 'Thanks for waiting,' but I did not need thanks. I could not have left before the winning goal.

'Hail the conquering hero!' I said jubilantly, giving him 'thumbs up'.

He did not respond and suddenly I saw how white he looked against the tan leather jacket. 'It was touch and go.'

The realization filled me with compunction. This was no game. Clare would never have treated it so lightly. 'I'll drive, shall I?'

'Thanks, if you would.' He let me slide across and took the seat I had vacated.

We looked at each other for a minute. 'Dear God, it hurts, loving him like this,' I thought. What Martin thought I could not guess. He said briskly: 'Home, James.'

I judged correctly that conversation would not be welcome. We were almost half-way when Martin spoke: 'You must think me a goon, flaking out like that. Fact is I know my limitations. It's one way they were short-changed when they got me instead of my cousin.'

I looked as blank as I felt.

He smiled. 'Your man Hew – as they'd say in Ireland – is a natural with people. One look and they eat out of his hand. I've envied him that since I was ten years of age.'

'Are you serious?' Surprise made me breathless.

'Surely you don't dispute it? You of all people ...' I sensed he was watching me closely. 'You haven't changed your mind about Hew?'

There was only one answer. If Martin were to know that at last I had put a child's love into its right perspective, he might put two and two together and suspect who had taken Hew's place. 'Of course I haven't. Don't put words in my mouth.'

'Then you'll appreciate why I'm hoping he'll do a public relations job for me on Tuesday. Talk to the womenfolk of the chaps we're moving to Dunbeagle. There's a good deal of unrest, due mainly to ignorance. I'm confident seventy-five per cent of it can be allayed by a session with someone who knows and loves the place.'

'It's asking a lot, Martin. You know how much Har-esmead meant to him.' Would I in Hew's shoes make things easy for the juggernaut which had destroyed his home?

'Yes, but I also know Hew,' Martin answered calmly. 'I'll be surprised if he says no.'

At Chards on Sunday lunch was the main meal. After that Mrs. Trigg was off duty until breakfast time on Monday. Today, however, when we walked in the house was pervaded with spicy aromas. Mrs. Trigg said dourly that there was no use standing waiting for buses in the rain, so she had told her friends not to expect her.

A beef casserole flavoured with herbs came to the table with sprouts and potatoes.

'Hope you fancy a bite of something hot.' Mrs. Trigg's tone to her employer was almost a threat.

None of us was deceived, he least of all. 'After nine hours on a cup of coffee what do you think?'

There was plainly a lot more to Mrs. Trigg's dour exterior than I had at first divined. She knew where we had been and was patently relieved at the outcome. It went without saying that Dad was equally pleased. He had already announced his intention of giving a dinner party to celebrate the engagement. Now he told us it had been arranged for tomorrow. He had booked a table at a hotel whose restaurant was noted for its cuisine and since Clare had telephoned again just before Martin and I had returned it had seemed a good opportunity to ask her to join us.

Oh, heavens, I thought, the celebration had been embarrassing enough without that. Surely Clare would not have accepted? It seemed, however, that she had, and moreover that she had been delighted.

'Don't know when I've met a girl I liked so much,' Dad went on, making it worse. 'I reckon that husband of hers was a lucky man.'

'Very much so,' Martin agreed.

Hew had said nothing, but I could see from his expression that he shared all my misgivings. 'Are you sure you want me in on this, Jack?' he inquired suddenly. 'You'd have four without me.'

'And I know what Judy would have to say about that!' Dad chuckled. 'Time was when we thought we might be getting you as a son-in-law. When she was thirteen I was always telling her to declare herself!'

'Yes, well, she didn't,' Hew said shortly, his eyes holding mine.

'Of course you must come, Dad is right,' I answered hastily.

Martin and I were alone together in the glass porch for a few minutes after supper.

'Don't you think we should drop Dad a hint?' I whispered. 'Tomorrow is going to be desperately hard on Clare.'

'Oh, I think she can take it,' he returned coolly. 'You underestimate Clare. She's very tough. And we're dropping no hints, my love, that's for sure. Not at this crucial stage.'

Mrs. Trigg's good cooking had completely restored his equilibrium. It was not long before he was putting his request to Hew, who listened to it frowning.

Martin explained. Irish Iceberg was one of the wildcat grievances which Tom Grundy had fanned into flame. At present it concerned fewer than twenty men who had been asked to transfer with agreed disturbance pay. If the wives proved awkward the men might retract, and they were hand-picked and had a key rôle to play. In addition he saw it developing into a conflict which could affect all Iceberg areas of expansion. It was quite true that Dunbeagle was not included in the terms on which they were to vote on Tuesday night, but it was important that when they went to the ballot box no unsettling rumours should be flying about.

'I've guaranteed the negotiating committee I can dispel all doubts by the end of working on Tuesday. I want them to pick a time, morning or afternoon, when their wives can come in to the canteen, have a cup of tea and ask you any questions they like. What do you think?'

There was a pause. 'I think you shouldn't have guaranteed it,' Hew said slowly. 'Because I won't be here. On Tuesday I'm going to London.'

'Can't you put it off?' Martin asked urgently.

'Impossible, I'm afraid. I've an appointment.'

'And tomorrow would be impracticable from our end.

They have to make arrangements.' Martin folded his lips. 'Well, that's it, then. We'll just have to postpone it. When will you be home?'

'I've no idea.' Hew might have been declining a dinner invitation. 'I really feel in the circumstances you should count me out.'

There was silence. It had been said as smoothly as Martin himself might have spoken. The cigarette in Hew's hand remained steady, his straight gaze did not waver. Watching, I was torn both ways. Martin had asked the impossible, but the awful part was that he had counted on Hew's help. I seemed to see them as they had been twenty years ago, the one a tall twenty-two-year-old graduate with a father whom everyone respected and the other a small ten-year-old with divorced parents each of whom had moved out of England leaving him behind. Martin must have longed for a place in the family circle and I was sure Hew in his easy way had welcomed him. And as a result, perhaps, had been hero-worshipped.

The rest was still dark. What had driven Hew away from Iceberg or Trelawneys as it must have been in 1962? And what a terrible twist that he should have been connected with the company who had levelled Haresmead.

The thought of Haresmead evoked the picture of Isolde. From first to last it had haunted me. Perhaps prophetically, for Isolde had stood doomed between the man to whom she owed loyalty and the one she loved.

'What will you do now?' my father was asking Martin sympathetically.

'Think again,' he answered.

Dad glanced in my direction. 'Have you tried asking Judy? She's a dab hand at talking.'

As I caught my breath Martin said easily, 'No, I wouldn't ask Judith. It wouldn't be fair.'

'I don't know,' Dad philosophized. 'All's fair in love and war, isn't that what they say? And it wouldn't be the first time they sent a girl from Ireland to unite her country with Cornwall.'

My father had an uncanny knack of picking up my thoughts. It did not surprise me that he had done so now. Thinking, however, was one thing, doing quite another.

'That was a different kind of union,' I said sharply.

'Well, now I always thought there was just the one,' Dad remarked with interest. 'But I suppose you don't want to go by your mother and me.'

On my first night at Chards, when I was in no shape for the strain of meeting Clare, Martin had stepped in to save me. Now his eyes had the same understanding.

'Forget it, Jack. It's out of the question. I know how Judith feels about Haresmead.'

'Ah, will you wait now, lad?' Dad retorted. 'Give the girl a chance to show how she feels about you.'

My father was often at his wisest when he seemed meddlesome and rustic. I never quite knew how much of it was guile. But he had made up his mind for me.

'Why is it out of the question, Martin?' I asked. 'As your fiancée I should have thought I was the obvious choice.'

'My dear, I was giving you a chance . . .' In company Martin usually called me 'darling'. 'My dear' had a new ring. It sounded so true that my heart gave a stupid lurch.

He leaned over my chair and kissed me. I knew that I should have been used to it, but I wasn't. For a wild moment I even wondered if he and Clare cared for each other as deeply as I'd thought.

'I'm very grateful,' Martin said softly. He added for my ear alone: 'You must let me know if there's anything I can do in return.'

CHAPTER NINE

THE day Dad and I had gone to Truro he had said: 'And now I suppose you haven't a thing to wear!' It was an old family joke. I had taken my cue and money had changed hands.

I put on the result for the engagement dinner. It was an overdress, long, loose and belted. The colour was cream and it went over a matching shirt with a small black pattern. I brushed my hair out and left it loose.

My father was not impressed. 'And what class of a thing is that you're wearing?' he demanded unflatteringly when I went downstairs. 'If you ask me, it looks like a dressing-gown.'

'If you ask me,' Hew put in equally unfortunately, 'she looks like a virgin martyr.'

'Sorry, but I'm not taking it off,' I declared firmly.

'That's a pity.' Martin was not slow in taking his turn. He added enigmatically: 'Miss Gale has once more satisfied her public.'

It had been arranged that Hew should pick up Clare and Martin drive Dad and me. He took us down through Port Isaac and tense as I was I enjoyed it. There was much to charm in the old fishing village. Its narrow streets were steep as staircases, its walls were smothered in pink valerian, there were white hotels with pale blue balconies and pub signs reading 'Camelot' and 'The Smugglers' Rest'.

The hotel was two miles away, intimate and full of character. The bar had rafters, red and white plates on the wall and a stuffed parrot. In the dining-room brass birds flew along a coal-black beam. Red wall lights threw a glow on ruby drinking glasses and soft pink tablecloths.

It was a setting which Clare suited better than me. She was dressed mostly in pink; a new-length gathered skirt and a fiesta-patterned shirt. Her hair was full and soft and she wore a lot of jewellery.

When she came in she kissed me. 'I'm so happy for you both. And so pleased about tomorrow. It's a super idea. I expect Martin told you we've got it all laid on.'

We had aperitifs in the bar. Martin tried to trick me into believing the parrot was alive and Clare sat between Dad and Hew smiling at each in turn and matching all their jokes with the repartee at which she excelled.

It was the same when we went in to dinner. But was it possible to mask feelings all the time? If she cared at all it would show before the night was out. It would have to. *If she cared at all* . . .

The elation I felt was completely crazy, and yet – *if*

Clare didn't care the accepted ending was gone. It was as far as I would allow myself to look.

A superb menu helped the party along. Dad made a speech which astonished me by its wit. Glasses were raised and Martin got to his feet. After he had responded I saw his hand go to his pocket. As he drew it out again something flashed.

'A suitable time, I think, to rectify an omission,' he said evenly.

I saw Dad give a knowing grin. Then my hand was taken and Martin was slipping the old signet from my finger. 'With all my love,' he said composedly as he fitted on its replacement.

The ring was exquisite, a square-cut emerald flanked by a couple of small diamonds. On Saturday, window shopping in Padstow, I had unthinkingly expressed a preference for emeralds and, thanks to a little connivance on the part of my father, the size was right.

But everything else was wrong. The gesture was extravagant and unnecessary. Martin's tone and words came near sacrilege.

I stretched my hand out numbly for inspection. First Clare, then Dad, took it admiringly. Hew made no such move. His face seemed to have set in hard brown lines. Oh, I knew it would have had to come some day, but not like this, so public, so final, so blade-twisting.

'Again happy days,' Clare was saying charmingly. 'He couldn't have chosen anything that suited you better.'

I marvelled at her strength and allowed myself again that glimmer of hope. Did she love Martin or would she be just as happy to see him happily settled? I knew it would give me pleasure if Hew were to find the right girl.

Meantime there was Martin. 'Are you mad?' I whispered. 'I don't want this. I have a ring.'

'You're rocking the boat, my dove. Please to stay still,' he whispered back.

My eyes were on Clare. She had gone very pale and Hew had said something to her. I was sure her lips had framed something like: 'I'm all right.' He laid his hand unobtrusively over hers.

'Before we leave,' Martin said quietly, 'may I give you a final toast. Judith the brave! Untamed and unsurpassed!'

The blood rushed to my cheeks. The raised red glasses seemed to be coming at me. The words Martin had spoken sang in my ears. I was being given everything – and nothing, and I couldn't bear it. Nor could I look away from those dark deliberate eyes.

I think I would have cracked if at that moment Clare had not set down her glass. 'Would you excuse me, Jack? You won't think me rude . . .

'A bit of a headache,' she admitted as Hew went to claim her coat. 'You do understand?'

'Of course, of course. Can we get you anything?' my father offered concernedly.

'Nothing at all, thanks. I've plenty of dope at home,' Clare said lightly. 'And please don't let me break up the party. I'm sure I can phone for a taxi.'

Predictably, however, Hew insisted on driving her home.

'Don't you think *you* could have done that?' I challenged Martin.

He could not understand how I felt, raw with pain and agonized disappointment. He was not to know the idiotic straws I had grasped at.

Now he answered smoothly, 'It would be quite out of place. We don't want to make them suspicious.'

'Suspicious?' I flared. 'Is that all you can think of? This ridiculous charade? Didn't you see her face? Do you care for her at all?'

'Unquestionably.' He answered the last question first, keeping his eye out for my father who had gone to the door with his departing guests. 'But within bounds. Clare will never marry me.' He said it calmly, even with a twinkle.

I blinked incredulously. 'But if you know that, why all this pretence? Why me?'

'The game is never lost till the final whistle. I've just scored a goal,' he replied with satisfaction.

'And yet you say Clare will never marry you?'

'Marriage, to me, is not the point at issue.' He looked at

my silent face. 'Believe me, there were good reasons for letting you think otherwise. You had to be fully committed and you might have found that difficult, knowing the truth.'

'Times change. I don't think I've ever found that especially difficult to face.' My throat had gone dry.

'I wish you meant that.' He paused. 'Judith, I appreciate you've been kept in the dark, but not for much longer, I promise.' The deep concern in his voice was akin to patting me on the head.

'For goodness' sake don't labour the point,' I snapped. 'I understand perfectly. I wasn't born yesterday.'

It was also crystal clear that I should have spotted it long ago. As Martin had just said, to him marriage was not an important thing. This apart, the situation was unchanged. He wanted Clare and had used me to break down her resistance. She had shown him now how desperately she cared. He would use that advantage according to his pleasure.

The game was as old as Adam and Martin was a more dangerous player than most. He was certainly the first man whose lovemaking I had ever desired. But now that I knew him for what he was, specious, arrogant and cruel, it was time to make my position clear – more than time, since Dad would soon be returning.

'Martin, I must say something. Perhaps it's stating the obvious, but I don't love you. In case that's too old-fashioned, you don't turn me on.'

'Thank you. I don't need it spelled out.' His face had whitened.

'So long as we understand each other,' I said amiably. 'It was just – I got a fright. You played your part so well.'

'And you yours,' he flashed.

For all my bitter disappointment I felt a pang. Even in its death throes love was not powerless.

I drew a patient breath. 'Yes. I did it for Clare, of course. I'm concerned to make my point, Martin. At times I think we both went too far and I don't want to leave you under any misapprehension.'

His eyes made it an uneven contest. They were so deep

and quiet. I longed to look away, but it was essential to appear apologetic and detached. I riveted my gaze and waited.

'You're a cool one,' he said at last.

'I'm my own woman. I've had to be,' I returned. 'But don't let's pretend. We're two of a kind. I'll finish the game if you like, but I think not with this ring. Here you are.' I slipped it from my finger. 'Returned "*with all my love*"!'

The mimicry was not bad and as he took it silently I dealt my *coup de grâce*. I looked at him as though trying to keep a straight face and then let myself bubble into laughter. 'You were so funny. You should have seen yourself. That kind of thing went out with Charles Boyer!'

I had often joked about 'this hurts me more than it does you'. The moment taught me how true it could be. I had wounded Martin, yes, but I felt that I myself was about to shrivel. It was surely not possible to go on living with the echo of the jibes I'd uttered.

Nothing, however, struck me into oblivion.

Dad came along at that moment and I heard myself speak quite normally: 'I had to take off my ring. It was a little too big and I wouldn't risk it. Martin is going to take it back to the shop.'

The night had one more incident. Dad reported that Hew had asked us not to go to bed before he got in as there was something he wanted to tell us.

He arrived while I was in the kitchen heating the coffee Mrs. Trigg had left.

'How did you leave Clare?' I asked, not looking at him. I knew he understood what had caused the headache. Indeed, remembering the way he had touched her hand, he was almost certainly in her confidence. Fondness for me, however, won the day.

'Not to worry. She admits she's been overdoing it. Shall I take the sandwiches?' He lifted the plate in question.

'So what's this news of yours?' I asked, following him into the sitting-room. 'Anything exciting?'

'Quite,' he replied laconically, and explained. Through an old friend in America he had been approached to join a ten-month lecture tour. The appointment in London next day was to finalize arrangements. He had decided to accept and might even stay out there permanently.

'It's a good idea,' I said warmly. 'You'll enjoy it. I'm sure you're doing the right thing.'

Clare's arrangements for the next day went like clockwork. Most of the wives had young schoolgoing children, so a morning 'get-together' was preferred. A car brought me to the plant about ten-thirty, by which time my audience was assembling and thawing out over the refreshments which had been provided. I talked and answered questions for two hours and as far as I could judge it went well. After this, transport home was available for those who needed it and Clare whisked me away for a wash and brush up before lunch.

'Judging from the sounds of mirth, you were a wow,' she commented.

Martin had wisely decided that nobody from Iceberg should sit in on the discussion.

'I don't know about that, but they were very friendly and one of them made a date with me in Dunbeagle!' I laughed.

'Jolly good. Keep your fingers crossed!' she commanded.

She laughed when I explained that I had intended ringing her later last night to find out if she were feeling better. Hew's news had intervened.

'Oh no! I'm glad you didn't. As you can see, I'm back to porridge. Actually I had rather a depressing visit to my sister on Sunday. I expect that did it.' She spoke slowly concentrating on the mascara she was applying.

'I take it Hew told you his plans. I think it's a marvellous idea,' I went on.

Clare was certainly doing a super job on her eyelashes. She had let the first coat dry and was now putting on a second. As a result she didn't speak for a minute. When she had finished she said: 'Yes, he told me when he picked me up. I wonder will he stay there permanently.'

'I'm sure he will.' I was enthusiastic about this. 'I think it will be the makings of him.'

There was a strange little pause. In the glass I saw Clare frown at her reflection. Then she laughed as though she found me amusing: 'I think Hew was made long before you were, don't you?'

Two girls came into the cloakroom before we left and Clare introduced them. They were both secretaries, one of them worked for her, the other for Martin.

Martin's secretary was dark, vivacious and very pretty. She had lovely legs and she walked like a model. When she confided that she used to work for an agency and that after a few weeks as a temp at Iceberg Martin had suggested that she join them permanently I thought sourly that I was not in the least surprised.

'Would it be fair to ask you what you've decided?' Clare was rubbing lotion into her hands. 'She doesn't feel quite settled here yet,' she explained to me.

'I don't know Mrs. Weston,' Martin's secretary replied. 'I might stay over the holidays if you need me, but I think I'll probably revert. It's not that I dislike Mr. Trelawney, but he's not exactly your friendly employer.' Here her companion kicked her on the ankle and she broke off. 'My God, are you his fiancée? I'm terribly sorry.'

'There didn't seem anything to be sorry for,' I pointed out, grinning.

Silly and indiscreet as the conversation had been, it had cheered me, though I couldn't think why.

'That child is a cheeky monkey,' Clare pronounced as we went upstairs. 'But the best typist we've got. Martin has an eye for that sort of talent.'

We were a party of six for lunch, Martin and Peter Harcourt, two other executives, Clare and myself. It was a pleasant meal with Martin presiding benignly. He and I had hardly exchanged two words since last night, now he congratulated me on my efforts and when lunch was over asked me to go along to his office. Peter Harcourt accompanied us. He set the ball rolling by saying that he had seen my designs and was most impressed.

It was balm. I had thought hard and worked hard and here was the proof I needed. It might appear too early to be sure, but I seemed to know that I had my niche.

Peter Harcourt talked amusingly about my precursors in the field, dropping names like 'Quaker' Pegg from Derby and Jeffrey O'Neale who had worked at Chelsea.

It was not until he mentioned that I would liaise with the shape designer and the printers and said he would arrange for me to spend time with the latter in order to appreciate the problems that went with transfer making that I realized where all this was heading.

'Are you offering me a job?' I asked dazedly.

'I imagine he'd have something to say if I offered you anything else,' Peter joked with a glance at Martin, who hastened to affirm that intentions were 'strictly honourable'. I would join the payroll as assistant designer. He indicated a salary which was more than generous.

I had no words. It was wildly unexpected, the last thing I had ever thought of. My previous notions had been on a freelance basis. Martin's offer was not only more remunerative but a far greater showcase. In a group like Iceberg new fields would open constantly and with maximum publicity – in fact international publicity.

I took a second to consider the dazzling horizons before I shook my head.

'I never dreamed of this. I'm sorry.'

'Oh, come on!' Peter obviously thought I had the future in mind. 'Don't tell me he's got a thing about working wives!' He winked and looked at Martin.

The future was much in my mind, but not in the way he thought. In weeks if not days my 'engagement' would be terminated. It would be out of the question to remain where I could see Martin, let alone have daily contact with him.

Naturally Peter was at a loss to fathom me.

'We'll have a think about it,' Martin said with another of his not so rare flashes of understanding. 'I have an idea I know what the trouble is.'

Peter took his departure and we were left alone.

'Cigarette?' Martin offered.

I hardly ever smoked, but the need to steady my nerves was great.

'I know what's worrying you, of course,' he said calmly. 'But this appointment would be good for both sides. An adult approach is essential.'

'I'm being completely adult,' I retorted.

'I don't think so. In fact I think you're taking a most

exaggerated view. How many divorced couples continue to meet as friends?'

'That's different.'

'Exactly. For one thing we haven't got as far, for another, and more important, your emotions are not engaged. I don't turn you on, remember.' Arrogant as he was, I knew the phrase had stung. 'So all we're talking about here is a vague feeling of awkwardness in the sense that people may be curious to see how we behave. I put it to you, my dear, that it's not enough. A mountain out of a molehill, a nine days' wonder. That's just about how long it will take this place to forget we were ever engaged. Believe me, I know human nature.' He took up the piskie I had bought him in Padstow and toyed with it absently. I thought, as absently, that the sooner we broke the engagement the sooner he would be able to throw it away. It was a frippery thing, quite absurd beside the beautiful hand-carved bull. And how smooth and specious to call me 'my dear'!

'It's out of the question,' I said.

The thought of it set my nerves at screaming point. All I knew about Martin had after all not been enough to kill my love for him. Much as I distrusted his mode of operation, I still ached for what could not be.

It would be crazy indeed to invite this kind of danger. I needed surgery. My only hope was to be cut away.

'I had hoped you were beginning to come to grips with us,' Martin said gently. 'You've helped Iceberg today and I'm very grateful. I confess I had taken it as an augury for the future.'

'No.' I shook my head. It was not true, but at least it provided an avenue.

'Judith,' he sighed, 'stop running. We'll be in Dunbeagle next year.'

'I won't be,' I said flatly. 'Dad is fine. I came home to make sure he didn't need me and that's it. I shall probably go back to where I started – London!'

'Are you sure you don't mean America?' All the kindly persuasion had vanished, Martin's tone was icy.

'No, I'm not sure,' I retorted angrily. 'It's a free country.'

'In that case there's nothing more to be said. Except that you *shall* be free the moment I deem it politic. Two weeks at the most, I'd say, and in the meantime we carry on. Agreed?'

'Agreed,' I said evenly.

It was late that night when the news of the voting came in. There was a four-to-one majority for acceptance and the grapevine had it that the objections to moving to Ireland had been dropped. Next day Martin declared that he felt the need to unwind and suggested that we all went away for the week-end.

He had a cottage on the Channel coast a little out of Fowey. My father was going home on Monday and this was an added incentive. Martin regretted that he had not been as good a host as he had intended. Factory affairs had claimed so much of his time, and Hew's take-off to London had been the last straw.

I had a feeling he meant it, despite Dad's truthful protests that he had enjoyed every minute. There was absolutely no doubt about how well those two got on.

As for my own plans, it didn't seem that I could travel with Dad on Monday because the local businessmen's institute was sponsoring a charity ball on Tuesday and it was taken for granted I would attend it with Martin. Friday seemed the soonest I could conveniently leave St. Keir and after that I supposed the engagement would peter out.

The plan for the week-end, however, was exciting. It was decided that we should go down to the cottage on Friday evening and come home fairly early on Sunday to give my father a breathing space before his journey next day. No doubt it was childish, but I was looking forward to it immensely.

The ball I was dreading. It came into the category of all the other things I had found such a strain, my first visit to the works, the discussion with the dissenting wives and, most traumatic of all, the engagement dinner. Besides, now I could say with truth, and not as the old-time family joke, that I had nothing to wear?

'Something might be done about that,' Dad remarked.

'If I were let have a say in the purchase.'

'You mean you'd come into the shop?' I mocked, not trusting my ears. 'You with a lot of women trying on clothes!' In the past, Mummy had found it impossible to get him as far as a shop window.

'And why not?' he retorted, glancing at me over the stem of his pipe. 'Haven't I seen enough of them without their clothes?'

He really had a bee in his bonnet about that dress.

'Would it be too much to ask that you'd try looking pretty?' he demanded as we drove to Truro next day. 'You always did when your mother bought your clothes. I remember the time she got you a blue dress for a party, kind of a sky blue. You had a bit of flesh on you then and you knocked spots off everyone in the room.'

So now I knew what we were heading for. Sky blue! It was a colour I'd finished with at fifteen.

Eventually we made the purchase and returned to Chards. Martin was not yet in and Clare telephoned 'to make arrangements for tomorrow'.

'What arrangements?' I asked stupidly.

'What we'll bring with us,' she said briskly. 'It's not much fun chasing round the shops the moment we arrive. I've made out a list of sorts, tell me if you think I've forgotten anything.'

It dawned slowly. Clare was talking about provisions for the week-end. *She was coming too.*

Fortunately I was much better at covering up than I had been ten days ago. She had no idea of the ridiculous disappointment I felt as we discussed the menu.

'Clare is making sure we won't starve,' I said lightly at dinner.

'She phoned, then? Good,' Martin responded. 'I managed to persuade her to join us.'

'Did it take a lot of doing?' my father chuckled.

'Actually yes. But it's a feather in your cap darling.' He looked at me smiling. 'She's coming to keep you company.'

It was only a small cottage, 'one up, one down.' The 'one up' contained a double bed. My father and he would put up for the two nights in a pub he knew.

'I didn't want to leave you on your own,' he concluded kindly.

'You should have consulted me,' I said stiffly. 'It was quite unnecessary for Clare to come on my account.'

Dad stepped in at once. 'Now, now, everyone was thinking of everyone else. Don't let's scrap about it. The break will do Clare good.'

CHAPTER TEN

FRIDAY was fine, and as I had often proved, there is a chemistry about sunshine that acts on depression. By the time we picked up Martin and Clare at the factory all my niggles were gone. So, if appearances were any judge, were Clare's. Like Martin she had changed into casuals, navy trousers, espadrilles and a top and jacket striped in navy and white. She looked gay and charming.

We drove into St. Austell and took a road which skirted Carlyon Bay. The ornamental trees, shaven green slopes and still blue sea had a continental air, but when we turned out on the A3082 with its thick hedges of meadowsweet everything seemed more English.

Just above Fowey Martin stopped to show us the view across to Polruan on the other side of the Fowey estuary.

I gazed entranced at the panorama – dead calm sea, candy-striped spinnakers, old stone cottages in terraces on the cliff. The river was wide at this point and the harbour was crowded with shipping. China clay went out from here to all parts of the world, but the pleasure craft were more picturesque. Most of them bobbed at anchor with sails down, their red, blue and yellow hulls beading the blue-green water, but a few were coming in with billowing orange rig spinnakers.

Martin drove on. We came to a cove ginger-sanded, stone-cliffed, splashed with rhododendrons.

'We'll have a swim here tomorrow,' he promised. 'And I'll show you a smugglers' cave.'

'Swim yes, cave no,' I answered firmly. It was several

years since I had got lost in a cave in Yorkshire, but I had only to think of it to feel the old horror.

The pretty cove had lain in a well of green vegetation. As we travelled, this climbed back on the cliffs. Below us on the left the sea was a cooler blue washing against grey-green walls. Seabirds floated on the steel blue water and the rocking boats were much less highly coloured. The sun picked out whitewash and mossy roofs and old iron ladders.

'Oh, do let Martin's cottage be one of these,' I thought childishly.

As though in answer I felt the car slow.

'I must warn you two plutocrats,' Martin announced, 'this is a very simple place.'

The cottage was small and very old. It perched in a niche of cliff as though clinging by its toenails. We had to go down steps from the road to reach its patch of front garden and a further steep flight went down to the sea wall. It was the shape of an up-ended carton and it was whitewashed. It had a white door and square-paned casement windows and there were flowers growing along the top of its wall.

But its chief charm was its situation; it was the nearest I had ever come to living on a boat.

Inside, it was clean and dry and quite comfortable, but Martin had not gone in for any special colour schemes. It seemed to be just what he called it, 'a bachelor pad exclusively for unwinding', though he admitted that just after he had bought it he had taken a fad to live in it all the year round. During that period he had made a glass-fronted case to hold this collection of soldiers.

The years fell away as I looked at them. My old friend Darius was there in his spotted blue tunic, still bearing his spear and his silver shield. There were fifteen-millimetre Napoleonics, neatly moustached. An American in Confederate grey rode a black horse. I noticed Japanese foot soldiers that I had not seen before. And yes, there he was, and I was ridiculously glad to see him – the Prussian knight with his eagle feathers and his gold helmet and the tiny red pennon on his lance.

'I'm glad he's survived,' I said softly.

'Survival is his middle name,' Martin returned.

Without doubt he too was thinking of my last meeting with the Prussian and how narrowly he had escaped destruction. I had the grace to blush.

The evening was lighthearted. We drove into Fowey and explored its winding streets. It was a quaint town of porthole windows, blue and pink colour wash, and eerie peeps of dark water and seaweedy steps. Martin pretended to throw me down one and then told me about Cornwall's 'fair traders' and the brandy kegs concealed in the town's fish cellars.

'Martin missed his vocation,' Clare remarked as we got ready for bed. 'I'm always telling him he should have been a smuggler. I can just see him running a lugger across to France. You must make more use of this place when you're married. He really adores it.'

'I wonder what it's like on a stormy night.' I couldn't bring myself to get into bed. The effect in darkness was just as expected, you could not see the tiny garden and the plash of water was so near that it felt as though we were afloat. The night had a balmy breath, but I could taste salt on my lips. It was intoxicating.

'I never cared for it much,' Clare answered sleepily. 'I'm a fair-weather sailor. It used to terrify me.'

I wondered if she realized what she had said. Had it slipped out by accident or was it a way of telling me what I already knew? Either way the magic was gone. I put the curtain straight and turned away from the window.

The cottage sat so high that dawn was an experience. The white walls of the bedroom had blood red-smirches and the sun on the horizon was a ball of fire. When I woke Clare was already at the window gazing across the estuary. Her face was remote. Not much imagination was required to tell me that she was remembering other dawns.

As the sun rose the river mouth sparkled till it hurt your eyes to look at it. Seagulls brooded on the moored boats.

We carried our breakfast into the paved square of garden. There was pink thyme in the wall and I thought of Martin's song:

'Thyme will come soon and the red rose it will blossom, all in the month of June.'

'Penny for them,' Clare said gently.

'It was Martin's parents, actually,' I admitted. 'Does he ever see them?'

'Not really.' She toyed with the coffee spoon. 'I don't think you'll have an in-laws problem. It's a funny thing, you know, Martin has virtually saved Iceberg in Cornwall, but you could say he was a child who should never have been born. If it hadn't been for Hew's mother and later the old great-uncle who left him Chards, he could have spent the holidays on a park bench. That's of course what's made him so tough and self-reliant. He's always had to make his own way. But you were asking about his parents. His mother is in Florida, his father in New York. He went out to see them a few years ago, but I don't think they made the slightest impression. He went to a conference while he was out there and he talked far more about that. That's Martin, Judy, he writes off his losses.'

It struck me that she was trying to give reassurance. In a word, that Martin would make our marriage work even though it might not have been his first choice.

'Then there's Hew, another odd set-up.' I spoke my thoughts aloud. 'What made him leave the firm? Surely he should have taken over from his father.'

Clare gave an easy laugh. 'Nosey I may be, but I don't know all the answers!' She sat up. 'Come on, let's go for the papers.'

In the newsagents I noticed the proprietor looking hard at her. Finally he spoke: 'It's Mrs. Weston, isn't it? I thought I recognized you,' he went on as Clare returned the greeting. 'It's been a long time. Are you staying at the cottage?'

'Yes. Just for the week-end.' I had to hand it to Clare, she had produced such a casual tone for what must have been anything but a casual moment.

'And Mr. Trelawney? How is he keeping?' the newsagent asked as Clare gathered up the change.

'Very well,' she answered lightly. 'I'll tell him you were asking for him.'

When we got home she handed me the papers and waved me towards the garden.

'The men won't be long, I'm sure. Meantime I'm going to wash the curtains!'

In the past hours everything – and I did not except the curtain washing – had pointed to the fact that this was an emotive homecoming. I watched Clare sling the line up beside the white front door. She gave me a cheerful wave as she took down the nets from the bedroom and sitting-room windows.

One way or another there was abundant food for thought. I sat on the wall surrounded by the screaming gulls and hardly hearing them. When a voice asked suddenly: 'Where's Martin?' I gave a start of amazement.

Two small figures were standing beside me, the taller one female holding the smaller, male, by the hand. They were, I judged, about seven and four.

'When it's Saturday or Sunday,' the spokeswoman continued politely but positively, 'we can have breakfast with him.'

On the fringe of the world food crisis I sat nonplussed. The children were not so dumb. 'We can come back if you like,' big sister offered accommodatingly. 'It's not far. I'm Melissa,' she added. 'He's Dennis.'

The four-year-old looked at me solemnly and said: 'Good afternoon.'

I was still suffering from shock when a stalwart hail floated down to me. Martin and my father were coming down the steps from the road.

'You have callers,' I said unnecessarily.

The children ran to meet him and he took them into the cottage. Clare dispensed orange juice, Melissa invited herself to the cove with us and Dennis sat down in front of the glass cabinet and demanded to play with the soldiers.

It was a happy, silly picnic with a touch of fantasy about the hot sand and the magenta rhododendrons. Even the icecream, soft and butter-coloured, had a flavour all its own. We bathed and dried in the sun.

Dad produced pencil and paper and I drew pictures for the children – Dennis licking his icecream cone, Melissa dipping her toe in the water, Clare lying on the sand. Clare was impressed with her sketch. She retrieved it and asked me to sign it.

'Sorry it's not in colour,' I apologized.

Clare had tanned to café-au-lait, her swimsuit was white. Martin in trunks showed a hard gold body, slim but deep-chested. He came over and stretched himself by my side.

'You may draw me,' he said graciously.

'Class is dismissed,' I retorted.

For answer he took my hand and passed it over his face. 'Know me the next time, then. We'll hang me over the whatnot!'

'Hanging is too good for you,' I said gruffly.

A joke, I knew, but it had been disturbing. My fingers had reacted to the cool brown skin and the inky brows. I rolled over on my front and hid my face on my arms. He tickled my neck and reminded me that we had a cave to visit.

'Not me. I told you,' I said, vehemently shaking my head.

Martin expressed the need for a hand to hold in the dark.

'If that's all you want, man, I see four a-ready an' a-waitin',' I returned.

'That is *not* all I want,' he said blandly. The children were already pulling him to his feet.

I picked up Dennis's blazer and held it out to him. He grabbed it pettishly as I felt a bulge in the pocket. A big bulge, calculated to force any garment out of shape.

'What's in there?' I asked. 'You'd better take it out and leave it with me.'

The suggestion went down badly. The trophy, whatever it was, was too precious to part with. The round face went red and woeful. Dennis backed away.

'And *you* can take the grin off your face and exchange it for this,' I told Martin, tossing him his sweater.

He pulled it over his head, took the children's hands and marched them away. I sat up to watch him help them over the rocks which formed the right-hand arm of the cove. 'Sure you won't change your mind?'

he shouted.

I called back that I had to mind the clothes.

His were lying a few yards away. Touching his face had been dangerous, but clothes would tell no tales. Besides, there was no one to see. Dad and Clare had gone up the cliff to explore the ruins of a castle. I shook out the belted houndstooth trousers and the butter-coloured shirt. The sweater I had thrown him had been slate blue with Fair Isle bands in yellow, black and chestnut. A hand-loomed sweater. The tan jacket which for safety Dad had evacuated from the car was Cape leather.

All Martin's clothes had flair. They made my wide-legged red pants feel very ordinary. Martin made me feel ordinary too – continually.

I had found that the only way to meet him was to ape his only impregnable mould. But it was not the real me.

I folded the beautiful jacket and tried my cheek on its sleeve.

There had been no need to worry. Martin and his charges came back safe and sound. He persuaded me to look round the cove's rocky arm to the islet which contained the cave. Bays and rocky spits gave the whole coast a scalloped look.

In the heyday of smuggling in the eighteenth century the lugger would drop anchor some distance out and the small boat would go out to her from this very beach.

'That cave was one of the chief hiding places,' Martin informed me. 'There's an underground passage leading from it all the way through the cliff.'

'Not interested,' I said forcibly. 'Anyway, the tide is coming in.' A wave had broken lazily a yard or two from my feet.

'Yes. It does that quite quickly sometimes,' Martin agreed.

He chased the children on ahead and we went back to the car. Melissa and Dennis lived in one of the other cottages above the sea wall. We dropped them off and turned a deaf ear to announcements that they would have tea with us if we liked.

We were to have dinner in Fowey. The table had been reserved for eight-thirty and I was amused when Martin hustled us up from the jetty before seven and commanded that we bathe and change in double quick time. The clock in the pepperpotted tower of the parish church stood at ten minutes to eight when we drove in.

I think it was the colour of the river upstream that set the whole magic scene. It was kingfisher blue against the greenwoods that crowned the banks. Exotic, almost tropical with its piping of white sand.

Martin drove down to the harbour and to my surprise asked Clare and Dad if they were sure they did not mind being left to their own devices.

'That's quite unnecessary between *us*,' I pointed out sharply as the car turned right and headed away from the town. 'You have the most florid ideas at times. An average engaged couple would be quite capable of lasting out an evening in a foursome.'

Martin cast a glance in the driver's mirror. 'My dear, nature didn't endow you with the means of becoming at any time one half of an average engaged couple. I'm pleased to say I also lack that propensity.'

'In plain English, Martin,' I tried again, 'I'd just as soon have stayed with the others.'

'Then you must suffer with a good grace,' he returned. 'Because I have a fancy to keep this tryst without them.'

'Tryst?' I murmured uncertainly.

The road signs pointed on to Polperro. The Fowey was still with us but the country was rich, green and wooded. Young bracken fronds quivered on the slopes. It was peaceful but mystifying. I looked inquiringly at Martin as the car stopped.

'Well, Isolde, we're home. What do you think of the place?' Martin asked softly. 'That there is Great Hall.' He pointed at one of the fields. 'On the right, Chieftains Hall, on the left stables and granaries. I left the nursery for you. But come, my dear. You must be weary after your long journey. Let's go in.'

We were standing, he explained, on the site of Castle Dor, the ancient hill fort which in the fifth century, according to theory, had contained Lacien, the fortress palace of King Mark. The ship in which Tristan had conveyed his uncle's bride had landed at the Fowey estuary. Nothing was visible now, but excavations begun forty years ago and abandoned with the outbreak of the Second World War had supported the supposition.

I wondered how sure I had been till that moment that Isolde had ever existed. Now that I had travelled her road, she was as real as vulnerable and as troubled as I was myself.

Martin took me to a stream which local custom held had once been a lake which a king had made for his queen. We went to the probable site of the Queen's quarters and stood by the river where the jealous Mark had spied from an orchard on the trysting lovers. There was a creek with mud-flats where the combat between Tristan representing Cornwall and Morholt representing Ireland might have taken place.

I recalled silently that Tristan had killed Morholt and that at the time the Irishman had had Isolde's love.

The tight pack of tragedy was almost too much to contemplate. I knew how I had felt that January day when Prince had broken his neck. At least there had been seven well aspected years in between.

'Better a horse than a man.' Martin's intuition at times was startling. 'That's what you said to me. But you didn't mean it.'

'Does that matter?' I hedged.

'It made it all the braver,' he said gently. 'I often thought of you saying that. I was an inarticulate oaf, but I wished I could have told you how I felt.'

It was a dangerous moment. The correct accompaniment would undoubtedly be a kiss and Martin always did the correct thing. In my present mood there was every fear I might betray myself.

'Wearing your Tristan hat, I presume!' I joked. 'I wish you'd make up your mind! A few minutes ago you were Mark.'

'I told you once that turning to that last page is no way to read a book.' He flicked a glance at his wrist. 'The enemy is beating us, I fear. And we have a final homage to pay.'

We drove for a mile and a half to a crossroads, the Four

Turnings, Martin called it. A granite pillar stood on a rough plinth at the roadside.

'Come,' said Martin, taking me by the hand.

Nothing passed on the road and no birds were singing. I had an impression of quiet old age. The stone was ancient and crudely cut but, short as my time had been, I could recognize the stamp of Cornwall. It was bleak and enduring as the engine houses of the tin mines still scattered over the moors.

'Read the inscription,' Martin bade.

Five words in Latin were carved on the stone.

'Drustans Hic Iacet Cvnomori Filius.'

'Someone's son is buried here,' I hazarded brilliantly.

'Drustans,' Martin supplied. 'The son of Commorus. Scholars have identified Commorus as Marcus King of Cornwall and Drustans as ...'

'Tristan,' I interposed. '"Tristan lies here, the son of Mark." Do you believe it?'

'I see no reason to doubt it,' he answered slowly. 'It doesn't tell us much. I believe what it has to say.'

'It tells us that Tristan died.' In my head my own words of years ago rang their ridiculous jingle. 'Better a fox than a dog, better a dog than a horse, better a horse than a man.'

'Forgiven, acknowledged and remembered,' Martin supplied. 'A Cornish Prince.'

I stood silent. He had used the words deliberately, stressing the coincidence between them and the Irish 'Prince' for whom I had grieved so intensely. In the legend, Tristan had died in Brittany, died in despair at the false tidings that the ship bringing Isolde to him had hoisted a black sail as a signal that he was no longer loved by the Queen. Isolde herself, arriving and finding him dead, had likewise succumbed to a broken heart.

It was romantic and unlikely. People did not die of broken hearts. Most of them, like Martin, wrote off their losses. I would not die from my sorrow. But I was suddenly desperately afraid.

The colour of the river at Fowey had been unreal. The warm stillness of this moment was unreal. There literally was not a sound. Was something happening to time?

Could past and future have fused? Was I identifying so easily with Isolde because I had yet to share her greatest grief?

'It says son of Mark,' I said carpingly. 'I thought – nephew.'

'The truth will often out at the end.' Martin gave me an odd sort of look.

'Perhaps he never escaped to Brittany. Perhaps he was wounded by his father's soldiers and died here.' My mind put the pieces together. 'Perhaps Isolde just had to go on living without him.'

'Very likely,' Martin opined. 'But I expect Mark was good to her.'

'I wonder how good he was to his natural son?' I thought rebelliously. 'I wonder if Tristan had to spend the holidays on a park bench?'

'There are plenty of indications that Mark was magnanimous and peaceable. Some day you must let me put the case for him,' Martin said, laughing. 'Not now, though. If we still have friends they'll be two very hungry people.'

Next morning a blustery wind was blowing. It was impossible to breakfast out of doors and when Dad and Martin joined us there was a general lack of enthusiasm for the picnic we had planned. When Dad mentioned over-casually that a fellow guest at the pub had gone off to sample one of the nearby golf courses I looked at him suspiciously. 'You wouldn't *by chance* have got your clubs in the boot?'

He had and Clare chipped in to remind Martin that there were some old ones in the attic unless he had thrown them out.

The pair of them went off like schoolboys.

'That father of mine!' I sighed jocularly. 'The first thing he'll ask St. Peter will be the way to the golf course.'

'What shall *we* do?' Clare asked more practically. She put a folder of papers beside me on the sofa. 'While you're making your mind up take a look at those.'

I glanced up warily. She flipped the folder open and disengaged some sheets from the spring clip. I saw what looked like an architect's projection and the heading: 'Dunbeagle, Eire'. 'They're the plans for Haresmead!' I accused.

'Look at them,' she repeated. 'I'm going for the paper.'

I was glad she had left me alone. While I accepted that my previous stand had been unbalanced, this was still going to hurt. All my dreaming years had centred round Haresmead. I still couldn't bear to think of that glass and concrete box which would replace it.

For all that, I would be going in and out of Dunbeagle for years to come. It was probably better to be prepared.

I looked at the first plan and stared. It was an artist's impression of a graceful Georgian mansion; the windows were bow-shaped, the hall door panelled timber. There was a carriage lamp on the wall. Beneath it was written: 'No. 1 on plan. Manager's office and dwelling portion, studio, display room.'

I went on, haste and excitement making my fingers clumsy. There were factory buildings, of course, purpose-built, functional, probably just as stark as I'd feared. But they would be skilfully positioned. As far as I could see, building 1 on plan was to stand on the site of the old house. It meant, I reckoned dazedly, that what you would see, going up the drive, would be Haresmead made anew. There was even provision for modest pleasure grounds. The artist had sketched trees and pathways, little steps, a terrace.

'It's been the dream of his heart for years.' I had not heard Clare returning.

'Why on earth didn't he tell me?'

'Perhaps you weren't a good listener,' she said gently.

She would never fail to listen and to co-operate. She had remembered about the golf clubs, she had washed the curtains and now she was dusting the room.

'Here's something that should appeal to you.' She laid it on my knee. It was a wooden spoon, its long handle beautifully carved into a design of flowers.

'Have you ever heard of a love spoon?' Clare went on. 'Welsh legend has it that they were carved by young men

148

who had to spend years away from their loved ones. It was accounted apparently that the more intricate the design the greater the love.'

I fingered it thoughtfully. Clare would never set out to hurt me. I was convinced she had shown me the spoon only because she knew I loved craftsmanship. But I have never been able to spare myself. The spoon was a love token in the cottage to which she had come with Martin. I knew already, but I had to remove all doubt. 'Is it yours?'

'It was given to me,' she said quietly. 'I don't know if that's quite the same thing. Would you like it?'

'No!' I put the spoon down as though I were holding a snake. 'It's yours. Keep it.' I glanced at the rest of the contents of the case, and what I saw switched off all thoughts of self. 'Clare, have you got the Prussian? He's not there.'

Clare looked blank and asked which one that was. I thought she would have known, but that was immaterial. Any ornaments she had dusted were back in their places. But there was no trace of the warrior with the folded eagle wings.

'He was there yesterday,' I muttered. 'I saw Dennis playing – oh no!'

The same thought had occurred to us both.

'I think *"oh yes"*!' Clare said briskly. 'Come on.'

We hurried up the cliff to the children's home and drew a discouraging blank. Dennis, when questioned, shook his head till it looked as though it might drop off. Melissa quite obviously knew nothing about the model and their mother, though sympathetic, was positive that it had not come into their house. She had just 'tidied the place up a bit' and would certainly have found it.

When we got back I fretted ineffectually round the cottage.

'Cheer up, it's not the end of the world,' Clare consoled. I could see she accepted Dennis's denial, frankly I did not.

'He had something in his pocket yesterday at the cove and he wouldn't let me see what it was,' I suddenly remembered. 'I think we should go and look.'

'All right,' Clare agreed. 'When they come back with the car.'

'We can't wait that long. It might get picked up in the meantime.'

'It probably has by now, or washed out to sea. I'm not really sure how far up the tide comes.'

It was reasonable, but I was impatient. Where we had sunbathed the sand had looked as though it never got wet.

'I'm going,' I said impulsively. 'You needn't come.'

Clare looked at her watch. 'If only we knew when they'd be back ...'

'Wait here and tell them. Then they can come and get me.'

'All right,' she said reluctantly. 'I'm afraid I might hold you up. My legs aren't as long as yours!'

It was about two miles to the cove. I walked quickly, hoping that the deteriorating weather might have kept the crowds away.

The wind was gusting strongly and the water was very rough. It hardly looked the same place as yesterday. I had rushed out of the cottage in a short-sleeved jumper and a denim skirt and I had goose-pimples. No matter, all ills would be forgotten if only I could be lucky enough to find the model.

The loss of any piece from the collection would be sad, but the Prussian knight still had pride of place. Besides, he and I had a special bond. I had not spared him for this.

It seemed a good omen to find the cove deserted, but the hope was false. I walked along the shingle and turned the sand over where we had picnicked, but without success. *The only place left to search was the cave.*

The small hairs on my back rose in protest. But that was ridiculous. I knew I must conquer this phobia.

I looked at the sea as I scrambled over the rocks into the next-door sandy inlet. It was breaking boisterously but still far out. Comparing it as best I could with yesterday I should have about an hour.

The cave was not as awesome as I had feared, its entrance admitted a lot of light. I settled down to my search, always keeping an eye cocked for the tide. So long as I could see sand outside I felt safe.

There was the start of a passage at the back of the chamber. Perhaps one used by the fair traders in bygone days. 'Jolly,' I thought without envy. If they wanted brandy that much they were welcome to it. The tunnel was pitch dark, a real rat hole. 'Not for me, thanks,' I thought, unless . . .

Unless of course Martin having told the children about the smugglers had shown them the start of the passage.

I went a few paces into the dark. My foot kicked something which linked as it rolled away. A few groping seconds and my fingers closed in triumph.

Back in the light I looked tenderly at the rescued. Horse and rider could have smashed to bits on the hard rock as they dropped, but Dennis's pocket was low off the ground and miraculously all they had suffered were scratches and a slight bend in the lance. The delicate wings, the gold helmet and the horse's dark brown fetlocks were unscathed.

I did a very foolish thing in the solitude of that cave. I spoke to the wounded knight in my hand. I said: 'Did you think I would leave you dying when there's room on my horse for two?'

Then I walked to the mouth of the cave and my stomach turned over.

In front of me there was still sand, the sand I had watched so trustingly, but what I had not seen or bargained for was that the tide had reached the rocky spines at the open ends of the horseshoe. Where less than an hour ago it had been possible to scramble over them from one cove to the other they were now covered by a foaming, roaring sea.

No need to panic, I told myself. I would wade.

I would not have been so optimistic had I known what I was talking about. It was not so much depth as strength. I had taken only a few steps when a wave all but sent me flying. I went another pace and the sea came over my knees. To go on would have been madness.

One good thing, the Prussian was still in my grasp. It

seemed all I had to do was wait on my patch of sand. I tried not to think that at high tide this too might be covered, but if it were there was always the cave.

Some minutes later I heard a cry on the wind. The gulls had been screaming and at first I took no notice. Then it came again and insistently. '*Judith!*'

I ran to the wet edge of the sand and looked up. A figure was standing on the cliff above my head. I recognized the dark head and the tan jacket. A hand waved energetically. I waved joyfully back.

Martin cupped his mouth. 'Are – you – all – right?'

'Fine!' I yelled back.

'I'm coming down.'

I was appalled. 'You can't! It's too rough!'

I thought he meant that he would be travelling by sea. In fact he came by air, or so it seemed as I stood looking fearfully upwards. It looked fairly easy as he began the descent, but half-way down I could see that the cliff was steeper and to my horror some stones dislodged themselves and came rattling over the edge. I closed my eyes and ducked. When I looked again Martin, thank heaven, was still there. He was much nearer the bottom when the same type of rock slide occurred. I could see his face by now and it looked worried. He braced himself for a second and jumped. It was a noisy, skidding landing amid a shoal of stones and it brought him to his knees, but he was up almost directly and blowing on his hands.

'You could have been killed,' I said jerkily. 'I told you I was fine.'

'It takes more than that to kill me,' he retorted. 'And speed was of the essence.'

'Not just being difficult, but I couldn't climb up there.'

'Agreed. It's much too dangerous.' He sucked a grazed finger. 'I'm afraid we'll just have to walk.'

'Walk?' I wrinkled my brows.

'Bit of a bore, I know,' he drawled. 'But you can put your feet up when we get in.' The dark eyes, hard as marbles, were giving me an unmistakable message.

I swallowed. Three steps into that tunnel had been enough. If I had not found the Prussian so easily I could not have continued to search.

'Right then, what are we waiting for?' I returned dry-mouthed.

The marble eyes softened. 'That's my girl!' Regardless of protests, he stripped off his jacket and put it on me. I could have wept for the dust and scruff marks it had collected on the way down the cliff, but it still held the comforting heat of his body. I stood while he buttoned it.

'I got him,' I said diffidently, showing what was in my hand. 'I doubt you'll think he was worth it after all this.'

'As a matter of fact he and this have a price above rubies,' Martin responded shortly.

There was no hope that we would be safe in the cave. In a storm like this the high tide would buffet into every corner.

I am not naturally brave. If I behaved well that day it was entirely due to force of circumstances. I had a cool, unsentimental image to live up to.

Martin led the way. He allowed us an occasional flash from his lighter, but seemed anxious to conserve it. Fortunately for me he was wearing a light blue sweater, one of his dark patterned shirts would have been swallowed by the gloom. His left hand was within my reach and I held on to it.

We could not go fast because we had to stoop, sometimes he would say: 'Keep down,' and then we had to lower our heads even more. The air was warm and stagnant.

In the past there had been a tin mine here, our tunnel was part of the disused workings.

'They worked in this eight hours a day,' Martin said admiringly. 'With candles fixed to their hats. They grew bent and gnarled and lung disease killed them in their middle forties. But mining was in their blood and few of them would have changed it for another occupation. Despite the wild tales that are told of them, they were men of courage and endurance.'

Once before he had fascinated me by his knowledge of old Cornwall. On the 'tinners' he was more eloquent still.

As we made our difficult way I learned that the streaming of tin had started centuries before King Arthur or King Mark. It had begun on the open moors and as it expanded and prospered it had gone underground. Martin described how passages had been tunnelled out under the sea and how sometimes the salt water seeped through as the miners worked. He mentioned the names which had been given to some of the old mines – Wheal Rose, Wheal Kitty, Wheal Harriet – and suggested that the men who worked them had regarded them as sailors regard their ships.

'Knackers' were supposed to be the ghosts of dead tinners. Their knocks and tapping were often heard when the miners first went underground, their tiny axes would sometimes be found in clefts and if you were foolish enough to go too close to them they changed into black goats and scampered away.

After this he stopped to flash the lighter. 'Spaghetti Junction', he said laconically. We had come to a joining place of tunnels.

It was, though I did not know it then, a most crucial moment. Several of the tunnels led nowhere and rock slides made others very dangerous.

'This way,' Martin said decisively. He turned the light on my face. 'All right?'

'All right,' I answered.

'Matter-of-fact as always,' he commented.

'You'll admit it's a fundamental situation.' I felt extraordinarily calm.

As we went along the new passage he explained that tinners were the first smugglers. Pilfering went on at the mines with the objective of finding a ship which would take the tin to sell abroad.

'Tin out, brandy in,' he summed up, pausing. 'We haven't much further to go now, so I think we can take a break.' Again the lighter flicked. Its spurt of flame was frail, but it showed me his eyes.

'This next won't be a sleigh ride,' he said quietly. 'But we'll make it. Just relax and get your breath.

'You can tell it to your grandchildren,' he added. 'God knows why we think they'll have time to listen!'

'Martin,' I said suddenly, 'you have time to listen now and I want to say Clare showed me the plans for Haresmead. Was it your idea?'

'Yes, but not the original. I was able to lay my hands on some old sketches. It's a copy.' The Haresmead I had known and loved had been embellished in the Victorian era. Iceberg's architect with Martin's help had gone back to the house as it had originally been built.

The situation became still more intriguing. 'What a piece of luck! How did you come by the sketches? The owners, I suppose?' I knew better than to ask outright, but I was still intensely curious about those mysterious people.

Even in the darkness I gathered that Martin was not going to satisfy me.

'Yes,' he said briefly. 'I was very pleased. And if you can accept it so much the better. We're giving it a trade-name, by the way – Iceberg Isolde, and we want a house-mark. If you have any ideas let me know.'

I knew the breathing space had been for my benefit. 'Shall we move on, then?' I suggested. 'I'm ready.'

His hand found mine and squeezed it. 'It's easier if we crawl.'

It would have been impossible to do anything else. The passage was so low that I nearly showed my terror. To keep my mind off it, as we inched forward, I began to dream up an Isolde trademark.

Hew's picture reduced in size? No. It would be too complicated and would mean nothing to those who did not know the story.

'All right?' Martin asked.

'Yes. I'm thinking,' I returned.

It would have to be a single figure, something that appealed whether or not you had ever heard of Tristan and Queen Iseult. Ireland. Cornwall. What else linked them?

It was an extraordinary place for it to come to me. A line that most people know and find evocative. 'They that go down to the sea in ships.'

From that second my design was crystal sharp.

'Make it a figurehead,' I said suddenly. 'With Isolde's face.'

Martin seemed to find it amusing. 'You – thinking about housemarks at a time like this!'

'You pretending that wasn't the whole object of the exercise!' I reported. 'Well, what do you think?'

'I think I should take my hat off to a discerning and practical woman who has made good her offer one hundredfold.'

I was nonplussed.

'The day we came,' he prompted, 'if you remember, on your way to Chards, you offered me your head.'

'I remember,' I said shortly. Every word of the conversation came back. He had been playing my emotions, panic had caused me to withdraw. The same sort of panic was now doing the same thing. 'I hope I've stood by it.'

'In every particular,' he assured me. 'You've been a pillar of rectitude, cool-headed, matter-of-fact and loyal. I thank you for it. I know it hasn't been easy.' His tone changed. 'Success! Another yard and we can stand up.'

For some time the air had felt fresher. Now it was cold and draughty. I wriggled the last few feet and Martin helped me up. We were no longer in the dark. I could see the state of my clothes, espadrilles that had once been white, torn tights, a trail of red piping hanging down my blue pleats.

When Martin said drolly that we might find a reception committee I was appalled. It seemed that before descending the cliff he had told a couple of lads what he intended to do, and they had promised to raise the alarm if we did not appear.

I had been through a lot, but the last lap was almost the worst of all. The passage had come out about halfway from the top of the cliff. An iron ladder had to be climbed to the headland. Again it was part of the old mine. The engine house crowned the tip, windowless and ivy-covered with its finger of chimney. The tinners had climbed up and down the ladder as they began and ended a shift. Some of them had gone out to work under the seabed. They would have climbed it, I guessed, in the dreadful storms that lashed this part of the coast.

Today the wind was strong, but at least the sun was shining.

'Up you go, I'm right behind you,' Martin commanded.

'Cool-headed, matter-of-fact and loyal,' I thought as I took the first rung.

There could hardly have been a more ironical citation. In the last two weeks I had been emotional from start to finish. I had hated and loved and yearned. I had been all these things all the time. Was it possible that none of it had shown through?

The iron of the ladder was beginning to cut into my palms and my knees were aching. I knew better than to look down and I was equally afraid to look up. I kept my face into the wall of the cliff and went on like a machine winding down.

The end came on me unawares. Arms stretched to meet me. Hands took hold of my shoulders. Someone said: 'Well done, lass. Easy does it!'

Hew's voice came out of a dream. 'Judy, thank God you're safe!'

I had no breath to ask him why he was there. His arms went round me, but he was looking over my head. I had wit enough to realize that his face was strained and gaunt.

'Clare?' he rapped, still holding me loosely against him. 'There should be a third,' he said urgently to the man beside him. 'Where's Clare, Martin? *Clare? Where have you left Clare?*'

CHAPTER ELEVEN

'But how could anyone think *I'd* go down a tin mine!' Clare had pealed with laughter over Hew's mistake.

It had come about so trivially that I could not be sure who had actually misled him. Dad and Martin had returned from the golf course, Clare had explained where I was and Martin had driven off to bring me home. Dad had stayed behind and presently he and Clare had gone for a stroll. Hew had arrived to find no one at home and, on asking round, had been told that 'the two ladies' had gone to the cave. He had followed and found the crowd. The message Martin had left with the two boys had travelled, some people were standing beside his car, some looking over the cliff, and more again had made their way to the old engine house to see us arrive.

'Oh, really, Hew, what a fuss about nothing!' Clare declared in the end. 'Get them a drink and then come and help me with lunch. Ready in half an hour, you two, I expect you'll want baths.'

It was so wonderful to be clean and dry with the added bonus of warmth and tasty food that it was some time before I thought of asking why Hew was with us at all.

'Just an urge,' he said vaguely. 'And something I want to discuss with Martin.'

We were so late with lunch that immediately we had finished it was time to pack up and start for home. Martin invited Clare to the supper which Mrs. Trigg would have prepared, but she declined. We set off, Dad and I in Martin's car and Clare in Hew's, stopped in Wadebridge to say good-bye to her and arrived back uneventfully in Chards.

It was a full house again for Dad's last night.

'My word, I'm damned reluctant to go,' he confessed as I packed his case. 'You're a lucky girl, love, as I suppose you don't need me to tell you.'

I pointed out that I would be following him on the Friday plane.

'Ah, but not for good. You'll be back,' he cornered. 'And now listen to me, girl, there's no sense in leaving it too long. Don't go thinking of your mother. She'd be the last to wish it. Have the wedding quiet, but don't put it off too long. That's my advice.'

'Oh, Dad!' I sighed. 'We'll see.'

Downstairs, Hew and Martin had been having a talk and I fancied there was a certain excitement in the air. No explanations, however, were forthcoming. Then just before bedtime the telephone rang. It was Clare. She had heard from the hospital in Plymouth that her sister was to be operated on next day. She would, of course, have to go to Plymouth first thing in the morning and stay over till the patient was out of danger.

Martin was urging her to put Iceberg out of her mind and stay just as long as was necessary when Hew took the phone from his hand.

'Clare?' he said masterfully. 'This is me. I'll go with you, of course. What time do you want to start?'

If Clare was to see her sister before the operation they would have to be on the road before six.

'You'll want breakfast. I'll tell Mrs. Trigg.' There was a strange look about Martin. I took it to be regret that he could not take Clare to Plymouth himself. Obviously it would be difficult for them both to be away from the factory without notice.

'No, let me tell her,' I said quickly. I had a conscience about Mrs. Trigg. It was the second Sunday running she had curtailed her free time to cook the evening meal. If anyone was getting up at four-thirty to give Hew breakfast I was determined that person would be me.

'Judy!' Astonishment gave way to a beam of pleasure as Hew's head came round the kitchen door next morning. 'How come? I was picturing you still in dreamland.'

'Time I did something for my living,' I said briskly. 'Besides, I've a message for Clare. Please tell her I'm thinking of her and her sister and thank her for all she did. I don't suppose I'll see her again.'

It was a slip. 'You'll see plenty of her in the future,' Hew pointed out. 'Since I assume you're not awa' to bide awa'!'

He drained his orange juice and I took bacon and eggs from the hot plate and set them before him. I was standing guard over the toaster when he spoke again.

'Can you leave that for a minute? I want to talk to you.' As I sat down beside him, he patted my hand. 'He's a lucky guy, but I think he knows it. You make a good team. I've thought so more and more, love, yesterday put the seal on it.'

'I'm delighted to hear you say that, Hew,' I faltered. 'When we came first I . . .'

'I know. Don't rub it in,' he said in the old whimsical

tone. 'I was wrong, desperately wrong. But I wasn't sure you loved him. That was part of it.'

'And you are now?' I forced a smile.

'Absolutely.' He cocked an eyebrow comically. 'Am I right?'

'Absolutely,' I acknowledged. 'Have some more coffee?'

Hew thanked me abstractedly. It was clear he had something more on his mind. 'Has Martin ever told you about Haresmead?' I shook my head. 'Then ask him. And tell him I said so. Martin is a square,' he added. 'He carries the past like a debtors' ledger.'

'Does he indeed? He once told me life couldn't be lived like that,' I recalled.

'I'm going back to Haresmead,' Hew announced abruptly, spearing a piece of bacon. 'That's what we were talking about last night. It's a long story. He suggested it months ago and I couldn't make up my mind. Now I've decided to and I've washed out America. I've had my bread and butter, not to say my gravy, out of Iceberg for years. It's time I stood up and was counted. You see, until you and Martin rectify matters, he and I are virtually the only Trelawneys left.'

He went on to recount, as I already knew, that once he had been on the payroll as a designer. Design would still be his special responsibility in the new branch, but he would also be managing director, starting in Iceberg St. Austell as Martin's deputy to gain experience before the Irish plant opened next year. 'Martin seems to think that knowing both sides of the Channel makes me a good bridge. Let's hope he's right.'

The prospect made my heart glow. On his relations with the people in Dunbeagle there was no shadow of doubt. Everyone at home liked him. Iceberg Isolde with Hew in charge would be no newcomer development. When it came to day-to-day pressures, however, I was not so sure. Hew was no hustler and I had never seen him get tough.

He read my thoughts. 'Left to myself, of course, I'd probably bale out when the going got rough. But this time . . .' he hesitated. 'I won't be alone. This is where you

160

come in, or at least why I must make you understand. When we first met, Judy, you were twelve or thirteen. I was thirty-three and a drop-out. But I fell in love with you. You loved me, I knew, as an uncle or a big brother, I loved you in my heart as a man loves a woman. Your mother realized this, I think it worried her, more for my sake than yours. The only worthwhile painting I ever did in my life was you as Isolde. It was the way I visioned you grown up and capable of adult love. When Wagner was contemplating his opera, he said in a letter to Liszt: "I have in my head a Tristan and Isolde. Since I have never enjoyed in life the real happiness of love I will erect to this most beautiful of all dreams a memorial in which from beginning to end this love shall for once drink its fill." '

'Oh, Hew!' Tears stung my eyes. 'It makes me feel dreadful. I was so selfish and greedy, taking Prince as my due, and then giving up writing to you ... but I had no idea.'

'That was the saving grace,' he said simply. 'Everyone else knew. Martin came out of the west that Christmas like young Lochinvar, determined to put an end to it. But you disarmed him. He went away wretched with remorse. Even then, though, the chill wind of reality was beginning to blow. When I saw you together, the right ages and the right temperaments, I knew that what I had to offer would never be enough. Last year when you went to Sydney I made myself face the fact that you were gone for good and that the next news would be your marriage to someone out there. I was here considering the Iceberg proposition when we heard Martin was bringing you over as his fiancée. At first it was too much for me, as you know. It isn't any longer. A man can love two women, Judy. Clare is an old friend and I think we still have time.'

I had been hanging on every word, deeply moved at this unfolding of the past. Now the walls of the kitchen seemed to be closing in.

'Clare? You're going to marry Clare?' All I could think of was Martin. He might be preparing himself for failure, but I was sure he had never thought to lose

Clare to Hew.

'Put it this way. She hasn't said no,' Hew answered, smiling. 'But she doesn't want to move to America. I think she'll settle for Dunbeagle once I tell her I've changed my mind.'

'And Martin? Does he know?' I asked dry-lipped.

'He may guess. Naturally I can't tell him till I get Clare's answer.' He glanced at his watch. 'But I wanted you to know, Judy, for old times' sake, and in case we're not back before Friday.'

Belatedly I remembered my lines. First thoughts had to be for Hew and Clare, and so far as they were concerned the congratulations and good wishes I gave could not have been warmer. Hew kissed me and said touchingly that he would never forget what I had meant to him during his years 'in the wilderness'.

'If you can find it in your heart to come to the new Haresmead,' he suggested as we walked out to the car, 'we might rustle up a few of the badgers for you.'

'I can come,' I answered softly. 'What's more, I've been thinking, before we had this talk and even more now. You know Martin rescued the painting and gave it to me. I'd like you to have it to hang in the entrance hall of the new plant. Then it really would be Iceberg Isolde.'

'Nothing would please me more.' Hew's arm went round my shoulders. He paused. 'It's no good, Judy. Martin might still not tell you and I want you to know the worst. You often wondered who let the place run to ruin. Tell me, did you never have an inkling?'

'How could I have?' I questioned, and stopped short. Suddenly I knew.

'Yes,' Hew told me positively. 'Yes, Judy, *I* did. Haresmead was in our family, it came to me in 1961. We were going to make it Irish Iceberg then. My father was very keen on the notion. But I was going through a bad patch and eventually I left the firm and used it as a bolthole. I didn't look after it and it died. Don't excuse me, Judy. I could have raised the money if I'd had the will. Martin would have done it, I know that.'

I knew it too, but at the moment it was not important. For Hew the winter was over, spring had come and summer, I had no doubt, would follow.

I, of all people, had no right to reprove.

'This will be better,' I said steadily. 'Now you'll make a proper job of it. And it's just as possible for a woman to love two men. Here's one judy who does.'

I put up my face and he kissed it, first on one cheek, then on the other.

We had talked for too long.

'Haven't you gone yet?' Martin in pyjamas was leaning from his bedroom window. He tapped his wrist. 'You're late. Clare wanted to leave before six.'

'On my way!' Hew called back hastily. He waved at us as the car skidded down the gravel drive.

I waved back, but when I looked up again at Martin's window he was no longer visible.

We saw Dad off from Bodmin Road just before midday. The train was punctual but crowded. It had come from Penzance.

Dad let down the corridor window. 'See you Friday!' I called, waving after the train.

'I was not aware we had made a firm arrangement about your leaving Chards,' Martin observed as we drove back towards Wadebridge.

'Perhaps I should have discussed it with you,' I said carefully. 'But it seems pointless prolonging this. I thought that after the dance I should go home and after a week or so you could put it about that we were no longer engaged.'

'Ireland seems more attractive to you now, I have no doubt.'

Ireland, in fact any place which was not St. Keir, was pitiably unattractive, but at the same time I had to get away. I couldn't bear it much longer for myself and once Martin knew what I knew about Hew and Clare he would find our charade intolerable. The least I could do was relieve him of my presence.

'Ireland has always been attractive, it is my home,' I said reasonably.

He would know very soon now. I could imagine Hew breaking the news when they rang with the report on

163

Clare's sister.

'Why not extend it?' Martin suggested smoothly. 'You've worked hard. Play for a while.'

'What do you mean?'

'Just that. You've been uptight for a fortnight. The pressure is off now. Let's enjoy ourselves.'

It was tempting for two things, the news he would receive in a few hours and my own instinct for self-preservation. We had been alone the day we went to Padstow, 'Mr. Magic Man' had charmed me then. I dared not risk it again.

'You're quite mistaken,' I said steadily. 'I have enjoyed myself. If you think I've been uptight I'm sorry, that's the way God made me.' In a way it was true. When I looked back on Padstow I saw a Judith Gale who had never existed before and I suspected never would again.

'Good gracious, I shall have to have words with Him. He clearly left the instructions out of the package,' Martin remarked. 'Lilies don't fold their sweetness all the time, no one would ever pick them if they did.'

'You know, Martin,' I observed, 'I shall get cross with you in a minute. This whole conversation savours strongly of intrusion.'

'Meaning one lily is telling me she doesn't want to be picked?' he teased.

'Meaning I haven't come to it yet. I'm rather a rational person. I like to see where I'm going. I know I have my foolish moments, but they're not the real me.' Make what you like out of that, I thought desperately.

He demolished it. 'And the real Judith Gale wants a life that's efficient, earnest and joyless? Poppycock!'

He practised what he preached. He had played the part of my fiancé with such panache that at times I had felt he was enjoying it. It encouraged me to hope Clare's loss would not go too deep.

'I am efficient and earnest, you clot!' I laughed.

'Too true,' he agreed. 'And too often. But thank heaven not always. Somewhere in your very sensible being there's a spark. Mostly quiescent, alas, but I count myself privileged to have seen it now and again. That's what our sad world needs, the spirit of romance.'

'I don't follow,' I said truthfully.

'I was thinking about the good loser,' he replied astonishingly. 'The chap who can go down laughing – he's almost non-existent these days. Romantic love is another casualty. Who would ever waltz in the moonlight now? As for you, Isolde, you'd be so busy looking out for the kingdom, you'd never spot poor Tristan leaning against the gunwale!'

The turning for Chards prevented further conversation. He let me out of the car, turned it at once in the gateway and headed off for the factory.

His words remained, destined to echo in my brain for the rest of the day.

'I was thinking about the good loser, the chap who can go down laughing.'

If by chance he suspected that he had lost Clare, this could be a veiled cry for help, the only kind Martin would ever utter. He might not feel much like dancing tomorrow, but he would certainly want to 'go down laughing'.

So for that matter did I.

As I had anticipated, Clare had two pieces of news when she phoned that night, the first that her sister had stood the operation well, the second that she and Hew were engaged. Martin's congratulations were warm and immediate. Then he called me over to add my quota of good wishes.

'Did she tell you this was on the mat?' he asked when the conversation had ended. 'You were alone together at the cottage. Did she drop a hint?'

His eyes were very dark. As a barometer of his feelings, one which I had become quite proficient at reading, they meant that he was upset. Troubled. Not as unscathed as I had hoped.

I could not say much to comfort him except these few bittersweet crumbs.

'No, she said nothing, but she seemed quite unhappy at times. I got the impression that the cottage was full of memories and she rather treasured them.'

'Naturally. She used to live there,' Martin said casually. 'Henry adored the sea. He lived on his boat every week-end, they stayed at the cottage all the year round, which was a bit rough on Clare who's really far happier in civilization. Henry's health began to fail when they were living there and eventually he couldn't manage the steps, that's when I bought it. Indeed her memories would be very mixed. I told you, didn't I, that she didn't much want to come.'

Astonishment and shame kept me speechless. When I remembered the construction I had put on things it made me wish the ground would swallow me.

Wonders would never cease. The next evening when it came to dressing for the ball Mrs. Trigg asked me if I wanted a hand. I thought she might have been disappointed if I declined the offer, so I thanked her and said yes.

Strangely enough I was going to miss Mrs. Trigg. She had unbent so slowly that I had hardly noticed it, but lately I had begun to feel that we could have become friends.

'You look a treat, Miss Judith,' she said after she had zipped my dress. 'Pity Dr. Gale isn't here. He'd be ever so pleased to see you looking so nice when it's his choice you're wearing.'

My ever modest parent, I deduced, had been bragging again!

I painted a soupçon of turquoise along my eyelids. The dress was ethereal, sky blue chiffon iced with flowers of different blues and spotted with moss green leaves. Its high neck and cuffs were delicately shirred. The day we had bought it I had yielded to Dad's whim because he was paying for the purchase, tonight the joke was on me. That romantic dress with its long blue velvet streamers was absurdly becoming.

'Now let's see what Mr. Martin has to say to us,' Mrs. Trigg observed with satisfaction. She marched proudly into the sitting-room by my side.

Martin was standing on the rug in front of the fireplace.

The chap who would go down laughing had dressed for the part. The wine-coloured velvet jacket and matching bow, the pale pink shirt with its embroidered panel, above all the slight touch of hauteur were instantly reminiscent of an *aristo* adorned for the guillotine.

He was staring. I smiled embarrassedly. 'Not late, am I?'

'Late?' he echoed. 'Are you *real*?'

To Mrs. Trigg's delight he came over and touched my arm.

'No, ducks,' I retorted lightly. 'The fairies left me under your pillow. Remember?'

'If I'd ever seen you before, lady, it's unlikely I'd forget.' He looked at me with such intensity that I felt myself blush.

The mirror threw my new self back at me. An afternoon spent at the hairdressers had resulted in piled primrose curls and a centre parting. Soft pink cheeks completed the illusion. I looked like a miniature in a Victorian drawing-room.

Mrs. Trigg withdrew with a final beam and the promise that she would leave coffee and sandwiches in the dining-room in case we fancied a bite when we got back.

'Have a good time, m'dear,' she instructed me from the door. 'You'll be the belle of the ball, won't she, Mr. Martin? I do wish the master could have seen her, he always had such an eye for a pretty face.'

'If I live to be a hundred I'll never be the master to Mrs. Trigg,' Martin laughed. 'She's a one-man woman and I believe she'd have died for Uncle Richard. You've made a conquest, by the way. Congratulations. It's not that easy.'

Somehow it warmed my heart.

As I took the glass he handed me I found myself thinking about Clare. She must surely love Hew more deeply than his tempered remarks to me suggested to have chosen him above such competition.

'Nor would tonight have been easy – for me,' Martin added simply. 'Thank you for helping me. There's just one thing missing.' He took the emerald ring from his pocket and fitted it on my finger. 'I take it you'll have no objection to wearing it tonight?'

Obviously he was thinking of the business acquaintance we would meet.

'Tonight I'd be proud to,' I said softly. 'It is a lovely ring.'

'I chose it for the girl I hoped would marry me.' His voice was quiet.

'I'm truly sorry that didn't work out,' I told him.

He seemed to glean something from my tone. 'Perhaps you sympathize from experience?'

'Perhaps,' I said shortly.

We had a long drive before us. The stately home, Pendragon Point, where the ball was being held was on the outskirts of St. Austell several miles further than the Iceberg plant which took the St Austell part of its name from the region rather than the town.

We passed the factory and I was surprised to see open gates, lights in some of the windows and an array of parked cars. Martin explained that the night shift was working.

We skirted St. Austell and came to our destination. It is easy to say I will never forget my first sight of Pendragon Point with the tall stone cross on its parapet cleaving a green-streaked sky. I hope it's a memory I may keep for ever and some day put on canvas. There it stood, a turreted fortress with a high tower boding over the gates.

I begged for a minute to fix it in my mind's eye, the thick parapeted walls, the windows, square-headed and lancet, and the shapely hexagonal tower by the main block.

'It's enchanting,' I said dazedly.

'Good word,' Martin replied. 'I think that makes us the enchanted. The spell, like all good spells, makes each of us see in the other the person they love.'

'Now what does that remind me of?' I questioned dryly. 'Two people who drank a love potion, perhaps you've heard of them. Tristan and Isolde.'

'In Cornwall they're never far away,' Martin answered. 'Anyhow, you've given me good medicine. Moping gets you nowhere. Let's eat, drink and be merry, for tomorrow . . .'

'No!' I interjected sharply. 'No, don't say it, Martin. It's – distasteful.'

He laughed. 'I didn't know you were superstitious. Come on.'

The charity to which the Businessmen's Institute were donating the profits of the ball was most deserving and this, coupled with the loan of Pendragon Point, made the ball a big social occasion.

The magnificent old ballroom had been opened up and patrons had the use of all the public rooms in the mansion. Painted ceilings, Eastern porcelain and gentle pink and blue carpets made a feast for the eye. The house had changed hands many times and it was unromantic to learn that the present owners were wealthy industrialists who had purchased it within the last decade.

During the eighteenth century, Martin told me, it had belonged to the local squire. His daughter Rachel was betrothed to the Collector of Customs, but secretly loved Tom Perran who captained his father's lugger when she slipped across to France. So successful and daring were the two Perrans that their vessel had been outlawed and for months Tom had been unable to risk coming ashore in England.

On the night of Rachel's twenty-first birthday a magnificent ball was to take place in Pendragon Point to which, not surprisingly, Tom Perran was not invited. The young heiress, however, yearned for one dance with her sweetheart and sent him a message that her maid would wait in the garden and smuggle him up the stairs to a room in the hexagonal tower. There she promised to join him. Since she was the belle of the ball, it was difficult to slip away, and when at last she managed it she had no hope that Tom would have been able to wait so long. His ship, she knew, would be hiding off shore and in some peril. To her great joy, however, Tom was there, and as they held each other in the dance her love for him overwhelmed her and she besought him to take her away with him that night. Tom told her gently that this could not be and with a final kiss loosened her clinging arms and disappeared.

When strength returned, Rachel went downstairs to learn that her father had bullied the maid into confessing the plan and her fiancé, the Collector, had set a watch on the bay for Tom's lugger. She had been caught by a naval sloop and in the affray Tom had been killed – several hours before he had kept his tryst with Rachel in the tower.

'Which goes to show that smuggled love can be a dangerous contraband,' Martin chuckled. He gave me a mischievous glance. 'Don't look so guilty. I'm not after *your* past. In any case, Rachel made the accustomed retribution and joined a Sisterhood. Tom kept coming back to look for her in the tower, poor fellow, but it was a case of find the lady, and he never did.'

'You mean there is a ghost? His ghost?' Martin nodded. 'Have you ever seen it? Is the tower open tonight?'

'Shouldn't think so, and I've never met Tom myself. You see, he's choosy, he only comes once a year. On the anniversary of the ball.'

'Oh.' My interest waned. 'When was that?'

'To whet your appetite for the champagne,' Martin said dramatically, 'it *is* the first of July.'

'*Tonight?*' Ridiculous, I knew, but my cheeks tingled with shock. 'Oh, I'd love to see into the room. Would you ask?'

'Maybe,' he promised lightly. 'Now come and say hello to some friends of mine who've asked to meet you.'

This was the part I did not enjoy. My false colours had never seemed so contemptible as tonight amongst so many nice people. I received at least half a dozen invitations, all left open for when I returned to St. Keir, and it was dreadful to hear the congratulations being heaped on Martin.

He, I had to admit, stood up to them just as well as I would have expected and raised a general laugh by saying that he had a rival in Tom Perran.

'I know she's hoping to meet him at midnight.'

'Well, don't dance with him, whatever you do,' someone cautioned me.

I forgot to ask why.

There was a deal of good-humoured comment about the legend. A few of the men said gallantly that Tom would have been amply rewarded for the risk, the majority of the women decried Rachel's whim as arrogant and selfish. To me she seemed extraordinarily real. What of the agony, I thought pityingly, when she discovered that she had sent her lover to his death?

Under cover of the fun Martin set a glass of champagne in front of me.

'With thanks from a grateful patient to the loveliest doctor's daughter in the world.'

Our eyes met and I dropped my gaze. Why his look should have hurt me so much I could not have said, unless it was that I knew he was not really seeing me but Clare.

The enchanted hours wore on. In my book moonlight has always gone with witchery and tonight Pendragon Point lay in a pool of silver. The air was warm and still and presently the stewards opened the French windows and it seemed to me that the last line of defence against the forces of magic was gone.

'You've really got this spell thing on your mind,' Martin marvelled. 'I shall have to confiscate your Hans Andersen.'

We were alone at our table.

'Does intense beauty never scare you?' I asked.

'Continually,' he answered, staring at me. 'But I've always liked living dangerously. As to tonight—' he replenished first my glass and then his own, 'we agreed we were the enchanted. Let's drink to it.'

It was funny how over the years I had remembered the golden brown back to Martin's hand. It showed against the sparkling glass as he lifted it.

'To you and me – we who are tonight such stuff as dreams are made on. May all our realities be as good.'

'You have a smooth tongue, Martin,' I tilted coolly. 'And now you're putting me on.'

'Not "off", as you said once?'

I would not let myself be rattled. It would be so fatally easy to show my true feelings.

'You put me off on that occasion because I thought you were taking yourself too seriously, that's all. This is a time for play, as you've so poetically pointed out. I can sympathize over Clare, but it's a divisive question. Why spoil our pleasure tonight?'

'A mere bagatelle in the circumstances,' he said dryly. 'But marriage to me was not the name of the game.'

'Yes, so you've said already. I understand perfectly,' I returned coldly.

For a second he looked at me blankly. I was starting to feel uncertain when the band began an old-time waltz.

'Our cue, I think,' Martin observed, and swung me to my feet.

We moved through the crowded floor to the terrace and down the steps to the garden. It was after two, but the air was still tropical with a faint breath of the sea. The bay was not far from the garden wall and one could hear the lap of water.

Suddenly I had the clearest picture of a small boat coming ashore and a dark figure racing over the moon white sand.

The waltz was still being played when we reached the hexagonal tower.

'You've got your wish.' Martin dipped into his pocket and produced an iron key.

The gaining of it had not been easy. The tower was closed to the public after the hours of daylight because of a fault in its lighting system. It was only after much persuasion that one of the domestic staff had turned a blind eye to the rule.

I abhor getting people into trouble, but there was no danger tonight. It was as bright as day. The tower contained four rooms, the trysting room was the topmost. We climbed seventy stone steps before we reached it.

It was drenched in moonlight, empty and so still that I felt it was waiting. Until that moment I had never believed in ghosts. Now – and I put it as best I can – I felt that the love that had existed in this room had defied time, just as, in the case of the young free trader, it had also beaten death.

Did he come back year after year? I didn't think so. That night both he and Rachel had walked away from earthly love.

Each in a different way had laid their life on its altar.

Something made me think of the words Hew had

quoted: 'This love shall for once drink its fill.' Assuredly that had happened in this room – for the last time and for ever.

Martin raised the catch and opened the window. Downstairs the band was still playing and freak acoustics carried and purified each note.

'It sounds better here than it did in the ballroom,' I said, astonished. 'Rachel must have known it would.'

'Maybe.' As Martin spoke a new sound cut suddenly through the music. It was the whine of a fire engine. 'I wonder where that's going.' He leaned out to listen. Another tender followed within seconds. It was a sharp reminder that I was not after all in the eighteenth century.

'I suppose you want to get back,' I said.

'I think we should first perform the ceremony,' he answered, leading me on to the floor.

In the blanching light his face had a strange pallor, his shirt was white and the soft velvet jacket had dimmed to a purply grey. It was crazy, but for the moment it frightened me. He looked as though life and warmth were draining from him.

Moonshine, of course. He felt reassuringly solid as we danced. It was I who had become winged and weightless. Judy Gale had vanished and become a part of him.

Then he stopped. His hold tightened and we kissed each other because we could not help it. I thought of all those moments in the past when Martin had kissed me. This was the fruition of them all. The words occurred again: 'This love shall drink its fill.'

And then as I soared like an eagle into the sun the thing I had forgotten came romping home. To Martin I was Clare, to me Martin was not Hew.

We looked at each other in a breathless silence and then Martin opened his arms again and took me into them, this time with the utmost tenderness. I was fluid now and nothing could have kept me from him.

'How beautiful you are.' He twisted a finger lightly in my hair. 'Like sunshine on alabaster.'

'Oh, Martin!' I had found my voice again. 'This shouldn't have happened. It wasn't on the prescription.'

'Even the best doctors leave things out at times and then the patient has to prescribe for himself.'

'I think this patient can handle his own case from now on,' I said breathlessly. 'Do you mind if we go down?'

There was a fragmentary pause, then his embrace loosened and I was standing alone. 'No, little dove. The prison doors are open. Fly where you will.'

'A bit dramatic!' I forced a laugh.

'Perchance,' he agreed. 'But you were bound, my dear, even if voluntarily. That no longer applies. From this moment you are as free as air.' To taut nerves there was something ritualistic in the way he closed the window. 'Come along. It's time I returned this key.'

We didn't speak much as we descended the staircase, but when we came to the door I turned to look at Martin and found he was looking at me. Before I had time to think I was back in his arms.

There were no words, just the meeting of our lips, the sweetness of anchorage and then the desolation when Martin let me go.

Another night, another century, but the same 'last time and for ever' love.

'Dear Judith,' he said softly. 'Thank you for everything. And now I must take you home. We have to talk rationally about ourselves.'

What could be more rational, I thought bleakly, than the view he had already expressed twice? His words had been hard but honest. For that at least I respected him.

The wheel had come full circle. Today Isolde was free and Tristan was determined to stay so.

CHAPTER TWELVE

'MARTIN!' One of the friends with whom we had had a drink earlier came running from the terrace. 'We've had a search party out for you. Bad news, I'm afraid.' He paused to draw breath. 'There's a fire at your plant. But take it easy,' he added prudently. 'The fire brigade are there.'

'How bad?' Martin clipped.

'Not sure.' It struck me immediately that the informant was hedging. 'It was a secondhand message from your house. Now what can I do for you? Can we give Judith a lift home?'

'Please.' Martin's acceptance just beat my declinature.

'I'll come with you,' I said urgently.

'No, there's no point. You go with Jim and Lucy.' Already he was heading for the car park.

I ran after him. 'I could help.'

'The brigade are there. There'll be no room for outsiders. Take my word.'

'Martin – take care.' My heart quailed. 'Don't drive too fast.'

He sketched me a wave without looking round and went on to where we had left the car.

If I could not have gone with him the next best thing would have been to start for home. Jim and Lucy, however, insisted that first I must have a drink. It had been a shock, they knew, but I must not worry. They were sure Iceberg carried good insurance. As for Martin coming to harm, Lucy accused me gently of watching too many Saturday films.

'By the way, where did you get to? Jim held on to the call for ages while you were being paged.'

I told them hesitantly after swearing them to secrecy. Jim chuckled, Lucy affected envy, a friend of hers who had joined us said tactlessly: 'Don't tell me you danced!'

'Yes, and lived to tell the tale!' I retorted.

'It's terribly unlucky,' she informed me. 'For the man. They say the bad luck always follows the man in your life.'

'We heard the sirens *before* we danced,' I rasped. The very noticeable kick which Lucy had given her friend's ankle did not help.

Past and present events were forming a dreadful pattern in my mind. Two hundred years ago Tom Perran had died through the whim of his sweetheart. Tonight I had pressed the man I loved into the same situation. I could not think of that room without a shudder, it had been so still, listening and waiting ... most of all I could not think of that moment as we began to dance when stagey moonlight had bleached Martin in his velvet jacket to a figure from the past.

Our way went by the factory. Jim and Lucy debated as to whether we would get through. There was no longer any disguising the extent of the fire. Soon after leaving Pendragon Point we were met by a pall of black smoke. Fifty yards from the plant a police patrol was diverting traffic. Ahead was a red sky against which turntable ladders and the men perched up on them were silhouetted.

'Ye gods, it's a bad one!' Jim could no longer hide his dismay. He turned the car as directed into a side road.

'I must get through,' I said suddenly. 'I must go up and find Martin. I don't care what he said.'

Jim was doubtful but kind. Lucy stayed in the car while he walked me back to the police barricade and explained my identity.

It was a sad journey. The stench of burning hung in the air and dreadful smoke rose like a mushroom cloud; someone said the oil tanks had ignited. The hoses jetting from the long ladders looked pitiably ineffective. More units of the fire brigade had arrived, but it was appallingly obvious that nothing could save the main block.

The buildings were old and due for reconstruction within the next three years. For that reason the installation of a sprinkler system had been deferred. The most that could be hoped for was that the blaze could be contained. The new blocks opposite were at the moment intact.

There were bright spots. Had the night shift not been working the outbreak might not have been discovered in time to prevent it spreading. More important, the fire drill had worked and everyone had been evacuated and accounted for.

I pieced all this together from what I had heard in the

crowd. The nearest we could get was the factory gates. Helmeted firemen were thick on the ground and every hydrant trailed a scarlet snake of hose.

'Look, Judith, I know how you feel, but you'll never find Martin in this, and even if you did ...' Jim was too considerate to finish the sentence. He knew I got the drift and I did.

'There'll be no room for outsiders,' Martin had said. Maybe he had meant it only in the sense of bystanders impeding the efforts of the fire service, but there was another sense, acutely painful now. In the past I had not minced words about Iceberg. I had called it a monster and a juggernaut. I had talked about rape and destruction. He would find it anathema for me of all people to shed tears at its bier.

I just hadn't the right even if they were not the crocodile tears Martin suspected.

I was on the point of turning away with Jim when I saw Peter Harcourt.

'Anything I can do?' I asked stupidly.

'I don't think so at the moment,' he answered. 'Just stick around like myself.' He had come straight from bed, he was shocked and certainly not in form for tactful speeches. He had said what came into his head. If there was to be one shred of comfort for me this was it, someone thought I had a right to stay.

'Where's Martin?' I asked.

'Don't know. Up front somewhere. With the fire chief, I think,' Peter answered. 'Gawd, it's a mess!'

Two minutes later with a deafening crash the roof fell in.

It seemed to release the last lever that held my self-control. As the shell of Iceberg St. Austell crackled in a forest of flame it seemed to be crying for help. Once I had detested it for the edict that would destroy Haresmead, now it too was being razed to the ground.

Haresmead had died before ever the bulldozers had moved in. Iceberg was in full productive strength, giving to the world things of beauty and usefulness. It had been looked after and it had grown. It had seen Trelawneys come and go, it had hosted welcomes and farewells. I knew Martin had men on the payroll today whose grandfathers had worked for his grandfather. This old factory had never lost the personal touch. It had a heritage like the Cornish miners of endurance and courage.

And now it was having a most horrible death.

'It's not fair, it didn't want to die,' I thought passionately.

I had once said: 'I could never care about a factory'.

No cocks crew as I stood there. I was not as important as St. Peter. But the tears coursing my smoke grimed cheeks were surely just as bitter.

I thought I whimpered, and almost immediately another whimper answered and a wet nose pushed against my hand. It belonged to the thinnest little brown dog that ever wore a coat. On impulse I kneeled down and lifted it into my arms. It was very frightened and it cried in my ear like a baby.

'Hey, that's Jumbo, where did he come from?' Peter Harcourt questioned. 'I hope Nellie isn't looking for him.'

Jumbo belonged to an elderly cleaner pensioned some years ago and always known affectionately as Nellie. When the building in which she lived had been knocked down Martin had allowed her to move into two rooms at the rear of the factory. She had been brought out when the fire started, Peter assured me, seeing my look of anxiety, he had been speaking to her himself, she was quite safe.

As he finished speaking a new rustle of shock ran through the crowd. I saw heads turn and expressions change. More ominous was the springing into activity of the ambulance crew who had been standing by. Their vehicle moved up towards what remained of the entrance.

At the same time Peter laid a steadying hand on my arm. 'Stay here. I'll be back in a minute.'

His face was enough. 'Martin?' I quavered.

'I don't know,' he snapped back, shaking his head.

I knew it was a lie and I went after him still carrying the little dog. By the time I had pushed through the crowd the ambulance men were getting two stretchers into the ambulance. The casualties were wrapped in blankets, but one was an elderly woman whose face matched her grey hair. At sight of her the little brown dog keened piteously and almost jumped from my arms.

It was a miracle of automation that I held on to it.

Martin was lying on the second stretcher. I saw only his face, unmoving, unknowing, taken away from me. I felt nothing as I looked at him. My heart was lying alongside him on that stretcher, but I felt nothing at all.

I lost track of the hours that followed. Peter had had to go back to the plant. He left me in the hospital waiting-room, my eyes pinned to the door.

Martin had been struck by a falling beam and was still unconscious. Nellie, the cleaner, had committed the arch crime. After being brought to safety she had run back, not once but twice, to salvage belongings. The flames had not spread to her room, but on the second occasion she had been overcome by fumes. Nellie's chances of recovery were excellent because Martin had been so prompt to miss her, find her and bring her out.

The nurse who brought me tea took time off to tell me that accident cases could be unconscious for days and then make full recovery.

I sat recalling that it was I who had persuaded Martin to dance in the haunted room where according to superstition bad luck followed the men. I remembered the quietness at Tristan's tombstone and how close I had felt to Isolde who had had to live on without him. I thought of Martin laughing as we walked up to Pendragon Point. 'Eat, drink and be merry, for tomorrow we ...'

It was tomorrow now.

I barely knew what time it was when the door opened and Hew and Clare came in. Hew took over the vigil and Clare hustled me home to bed. I had a fear that if I once lay down exhaustion would beat me and I might wake up to find it was all over.

This she disposed of in no uncertain terms: 'The doctor isn't anticipating a funeral, but we'll certainly have one if you don't see sense!'

When we got into Martin's car in which someone had driven me to the hospital the thin brown dog was sleeping on the back seat. I had almost forgotten about him. He was part of the bad dream.

After the initial surprise Clare said we might as well take him along.

'What did Nellie go back for?' I asked. I knew Jumbo the dog had already been brought out.

'I will tell you when you're stronger,' Clare promised. 'A lot stronger,' she added as though to herself.

Between them, she and Mrs Trigg bullied me into having breakfast and going to bed. I put my head on the pillow around midday and when I opened my eyes again the room was dark. I felt in some panic fo the bed-light.

Oh, *I couldn't, I couldn't* have slept the clock round. It was midnight.

'Hello,' said Clare's voice. She was sitting in the chair by the window.

As I stuttered out a mixture of bewilderment and blame, she came over and gave me a hug. 'It's all right. Good news. He woke up at three.'

'And he's – all right?' I faltered.

'Fine. But he has to rest. Hew is the only one who's seen him.'

I had lost a busy day. Offers of help had been pouring in from all sides. Hew had already looked at temporary accommodation. And there was also good news from the disaster area. None of the new blocks had been damaged, contingency plans were already under discussion and there was every hope that production could start in a small way in the temporary premises within a few weeks.

'Nothing like misfortune for showing how many friends you have,' Clare concluded cheerfully. 'There'll be difficulties, of course, but Martin has a team behind him now and that will make all the difference.'

'He always had a team,' I pointed out.

'Not a family one. Now he has Hew again, and most important of all, you.'

I let it go. Clare was in such gay spirits that it would have been cruel to hint at the future.

Mrs. Trigg had left cold turkey and a salad for when I

woke up. Relief had made me ravenous and Clare, I suspected, had not had a proper meal all day. We ate with enjoyment.

I inquired for Nellie and was told she also was making progress.

'Want to know what she went back for?' Clare asked, twinkling. 'First Jumbo's coat, then his bed.'

'I don't believe it!' I gasped.

'Quite true,' Clare assured me. 'That dog is her only companion. Its needs had to be provided for at all costs.'

'Including Martin's life?' I flashed angrily.

'Forgive her,' Clare bade me gently. 'Some day we'll all be old and liable to get things out of proportion. At the moment you and I have so much going for us we can afford to be generous.'

It reminded me that I had not referred to her own good news. I did so now.

'Thanks, Judy, I know you mean that,' she said quietly. 'I'll just say you don't know the half of it. Or the hard thoughts I had of you at one time!' Her eyes were sparkling. 'He was crazy about you,' she added simply. 'And I knew you were gorgeous and I wanted him so much.'

'Martin?' I quavered.

'Martin!' she exclaimed in astonishment. 'Are you mad, love? *Hew.*' As I gaped she went on more soberly. 'It's been a long haul, Judy, so long that I'd given up. One never should.'

As I had surmised, it was not going to be possible to visit Martin until afternoon as he was to be seen by one of the hospital consultants. Hew told me this at breakfast and tried to persuade me not to go home next day. Circumstances altered cases, he pointed out, and my father, knowing what had happened, would surely not expect me to leave.

'But of course you must stay,' Clare put in, horrified. 'Do you want to give Martin a relapse this afternoon?'

'For heaven's sake pull your weight, woman,' Hew went on teasingly. 'Now is the time you could be useful.'

It was a case of the ill wind and it did my heart good to

see him so involved. This was a Hew I had never known, Clare's Hew, I thought tenderly, and what a good team they made.

It was a strange aimless morning. I found Jumbo in the kitchen with Mrs. Trigg. He was no longer wearing his blue coat. The too large homemade garment had come in for criticism.

'Makes him a proper figure of fun, don't it? Poor little creature. I've a good mind to alter it while I've got the chance.'

'You're fond of dogs, aren't you?' I commented.

'Oh, I just love them, m'dear, I just love them,' she answered. 'We always had dogs here in the master's time. The last one died a few years ago. Oh, he was a beauty, a Labrador. Mr. Martin kept him, you see, when the master passed on, and to tell you the truth I always hoped he would get another, but somehow he never got round to it. Perhaps when you're married he might think about it again. That's if you like dogs, of course?'

'Very much,' I said tersely.

It is always the little things that hurt most. Somehow the picture of Martin and myself living here and having a dog made my yearning that much more acute.

Jumbo was looking interested and I took him for a walk. After that I had lunch and set off.

Some hopes at least were fulfilled. Martin had a private room. His voice calling: 'Come in,' was stronger than I'd dared to hope, and when I peeped round the door he was not in bed but sitting by the window.

As a small child I had been a chatterbox. 'Will you watch that tongue of yours?' Dad was forever warning. 'With the use you give it one of these fine days it'll drop off.' In the small hours of yesterday in the otherwise empty waiting-room I had talked so much to Martin that now I had indeed lost my tongue.

I had wept and prayed and told him how much I loved him. I had said it over and over again: 'Get well, my love, get well, my only love.'

Face to face it was different.

'How are you feeling?' I asked conventionally, clasping his hand.

Martin said he had been 'dismissed with ignominy' and would be leaving hospital next day. He looked rested and his skin was its own warm colour. He also looked unfairly handsome, dark silk robe, lilac pyjamas, cap of dark hair, long-lashed 'sloe gin' eyes. 'This flight tomorrow, must you catch it?' he asked austerely.

'As things have turned out, I think so,' I said composedly. 'And if you'll tell me where to leave the ring I'll do so before I go.'

'I'd like you to keep it,' he replied without emotion. 'You've earned it.'

'You know I couldn't do that,' I said carefully. The suggestion had been a shock.

'Just a thought. A lot of us owe you a lot of gratitude.'

'You once told me there was more to life than the balance of payments. Why don't you practise what you preach?'

'Touché,' he smiled. 'You are the exception.'

'Don't give me that,' I scoffed gently. 'Hew says you carry the past like a debtors' ledger.'

There was a pause. 'I rather dislike being discussed behind my back,' Martin observed.

'Not as much as I dislike being kept in the dark.' I was beginning to feel at ease. 'You once promised me a full explanation. That's all the payment I want.'

'Forthright as always.' Was there a hint of regret in his tone? 'And unavaricious. I would call that the story of your life. As to mine, I'll try to be brief.'

There was no way of telling him that it was the story I most wanted to hear. Or even that I was not always forthright and at this moment far from unavaricious. I coveted the ring on my finger for something apart from value. It had no designs on a rich future, but I craved a share in Martin's.

Never in my life had I longed so passionately and never had I been surer of the end. We would clasp hands and say good-bye.

Meantime I listened. If the facts were not unknown to me Martin presented them with a new slant. He talked goodhumouredly about his parents and with great affection about his aunt and uncle and Hew, the family, as he put it, who had allowed him 'graft on'. Hew's mother had been Welsh, warmhearted and charming. The bond between mother and son had been strong and her death in middle life had gone hard with Hew. Immediately afterwards had come 'the business with Clare'.

As long ago as that? Twelve or thirteen years. Before Hew had come to Haresmead. I had had no idea.

The usual classic twist, as Martin called it, had been supplied by the fact that Henry Weston was a friend and colleague and Hew had had a lot of hospitality at the cottage.

My mind was filled with compassion as I picked up the threads Martin threw. Weston always an awkward bloke, Clare's deepening feelings for Hew, the Welsh love spoon he had given her, the bittersweet memories of the cottage with the man she loved a guest under her husband's roof. Then the facing up, the choice and the break. For Clare twelve years looking after an ailing husband, for Hew 'the wilderness'.

A drastic alternative. He had set aside his entire future in Iceberg.

'I don't think anyone realized how damaged Hew was,' Martin responded. 'My uncle thought he just needed a change of scene and that in a matter of months he would come back and the company could move on the Irish project. Instead, as you know, he opted out.'

The springboard from which Hew had pitched into his fantasy of loving me was all too clear. I saw how each year real life went that much further away and dreamland took its place. But oh, what a sad and sinful waste of gifts!

'If only we'd known,' I said impulsively. 'I'm sure we could have helped.'

'I doubt it,' Martin remarked. 'After all, *you* were the reason he stayed. He took Clare off the pedestal and put you up in her place. That Christmas I came over to rehabilitate him. It was disaster.'

'You knew about me *then*?' I was diffident.

'Suspected. Meeting you didn't help. I expected you to

be – advanced. Instead you were the youngest seventeen I'd ever met. You were so fierce that I thought every day you would take a bite out of me. And you were so forth-right and honest that I trembled to think what would happen if you knew who was responsible for your beloved Haresmead falling to pieces. In the end, having met you and hurt you, I went home feeling cheap. From then on I resolved not to interfere.' He sketched the ensuing years with a quick light touch. After his uncle's death Iceberg had had a rough passage which the bank had helped it to weather, then early this year had come my mother's letter about Hew's depressed state. 'You know now what that was, of course? He was expecting you home and you'd taken off for Australia.'

It was only then Hew had agreed to complete the sale of Haresmead to the company and return to Cornwall.

'I know it sounds like matchmaking,' Martin con-tinued. 'But I was convinced the road back lay with Clare. I work very closely with her and I knew she had never forgotten him. The trouble was he'd got into a rut, at worse he was withdrawn, at best, indecisive. I had to nurse him along, both as regards Clare and coming back into the firm, but I was doing quite well until that night I walked into your house in Dunbeagle and there you were in bed with a kangaroo! And the other incredible thing was you hadn't changed, at least that was the first im-pression.' He hesitated. 'I don't want to offend you.'

'Feel free,' I invited shortly.

'You were still the same blockbuster that wanted to fight all Hew's battles. You'd been half round the world and you still hadn't sorted your feelings for Hew. And you were – are – far too beautiful. In a word, set down in Chards you were going to be dynamite.'

'You forget I was damaged too,' I said slowly. 'At the moment we're speaking of I'd had one shock after another – and it *was* the first time Mummy hadn't been there to meet me.'

'I know. I said first impressions. They were wrong in some respects.'

'Only in some?'

'Well, you're beautiful,' he said, pausing. 'That's

irrevocable.'

'Thank you.' It was my turn to hesitate. 'And in everything else – different?'

'Invulnerable, self-sufficient, fully mature. With the power to give and the power to put a stay on it.' For a moment we both seemed to be back in the haunted room. I realized he thought me sophisticated enough to have taken his embraces as a temporary pleasure. 'For instance,' he went on, 'despite the warm salutation I saw you give Hew the other morning I'm satisfied you have no designs on him.'

'In other words,' I slipped in, 'I'm brother to Martin Trelawney.'

'In no sense,' he said quickly, and left it at that.

'Well . . .' I shrugged awkwardly, 'I can see why you set up the engagement. You thought Hew might think himself in love with me again. It's flattering, but I'm not sure . . .'

'Oh, Isolde! You're quite sure and so am I. It would have been like seeing his picture come to life. Besides, if I'm not mistaken there were times when even our engagement didn't deter him from trying.'

'They were very gentle tries,' I defended. 'I don't think he really meant them.'

'He had a chivalrous subject,' Martin said briefly.

'I suppose you couldn't have explained to me?' With time running out, it was the nearest I could go to a reproach. At all costs I couldn't say good-bye on a note of discord. 'You knew I thought I was the bait for you and Clare.'

'It fascinated me,' he admitted. 'It would fascinate Clare too. As to not explaining, all right, I prevaricated. At first I wasn't quite sure how committed you were to Hew and how you'd react if you knew what we were really doing. But as soon as I knew you better I told you, twice I remember, that marriage to *me* was not the name of the game.'

My heart lurched. He had said it so simply. Suddenly my ears felt flannelly. How had I heard it before? '*Marriage* to me is not the point at issue,' or 'marriage to *me* is not the point at issue'?

A stress, a pause that I had not allowed for ... infinitesimal but all-important. I could not blame Martin, it was my own fault. I had been taut as a bowstring, so over-sensitive that my brain had told my ears what to hear.

'What's the matter?' Martin asked.

'Oh – nothing,' I said sharply.

There was no use wanting to cry from shock and confusion and regret over the silly way I had tried to keep my end up because, say what he liked, Martin must have cared for Clare. Perhaps he had forgotten what he had said about the good loser and going down with a smile on his face.

'I think I should go now, Martin. Sister asked me not to stay too long.' The moment had to be faced. 'I'll leave the ring in a drawer in your dressing-table. And – take care.'

I had expected we would clasp hands and we did, firmly and warmly.

'Safe home,' he said simply. He put something into my hand. 'Take this with you. Homemade like Jumbo's coat. No, don't open it now. Keep it till you get home.'

The neatly wrapped parcel was intriguing. 'You're a nice guy, Martin Trelawney. Thanks,' I said softly, and kissed his cheek.

His room overlooked the hospital grounds, so when I got outside I looked up and along the rows of windows trying to pick it out. My heart quickened as I saw that he too was watching for me. He raised a hand in salute, I returned it and hurried on.

In the car I dabbed my eyes with a tissue, knowing I must pull myself together before I started to drive. Martin's parcel, small enough to fit in my handbag, lay there tempting me. I opened it. There was a letter and more paper concealing an object that was long, slim and hard. I tore the paper clumsily and sat staring.

It was a Welsh love spoon, carved and painted, like the one Clare had shown me but to my eyes infinitely more beautiful. The design on the handle was composed of cowrie shells and red roses. In the centre of the bowl and so lifelike that I almost picked it up lay a single wild orchid.

'They were carved by young men who had to spend years away from their loved ones,' Clare had said.

'And the red rose it will blossom all in the month of June!' How often Martin had sung those words. I did not understand, but my heart swelled with joy. And then I opened the letter.

'My dearest love,

The love spoon was usually a coming home present, this one regrettably is for going away. You have been so honest about that wandering star, perhaps some day it will stop over St. Keir.

One advantage about an engagement preceding a proposal is that we now know what it was like. I cheated; I was in love with you from the night we had dinner at the Abyssinian, so my five-star performance was the most natural thing in the world. The unnatural thing is having to lose well.

Obviously at this moment the greater love is on my side, but I feel you caught some of the spark. Will you think about marrying me, if not immediately then within the next few years?

Please give yourself time over this one, my love. I shall be in Dunbeagle next month. If by any chance yellow ribbon is required for the oak tree, a postcard will bring free sample.

All my love,
Martin.'

For the number of times I have read that letter since it should have fallen apart. Reading it for the first time I almost went mad. I missed words out and had to go back to the beginning. I said things like: 'It's not true, I can't believe it!' and then I started to laugh. It was silly and marvellous and a miracle.

I swear I danced a jig on the hospital lawn. Inwardly, of course. Outwardly, I smoothed my hair, picked up my handbag, locked the car and went to accept the proposal in a fit and proper manner.

It was when I saw Martin still standing at his window

that the fit and proper bit flew off into the blue. There was an ornamental tree a few yards away and I was wearing a bright yellow dress. The fifty windows along the wing probably all had astonished viewers.

'So what?' I thought as I pulled off my yellow belt and tied it on a branch of the little tree.

'Why wait till Dunbeagle?' I called up to Martin's window. 'I cheated too!' ·

Harlequin

the unique monthly magazine packed
with good things for Harlequin readers!

A Complete Harlequin Novel

You'll get hours of reading
enjoyment from Harlequin
fiction. Along with a variety
of specially selected short
stories, every issue of the
magazine contains a
complete romantic novel.

Readers' Page

A lively forum for exchanging
news and views from Harlequin
readers. If you would like to
share your thoughts, we'd love to
hear from you.

Arts and Crafts

Unusual handicraft articles are a
fascinating feature of Harlequin
magazine. You'll enjoy making your own gifts and
indulging your creativity when you use these always
clear and easy-to-follow instructions.

Author's Own Story . . .

Now, meet the very real people who create the romantic world of Harlequin! In these unusual author profiles a well-known author tells you her own personal story.

Harlequin Cookery

Temptingly delicious dishes, plain and fancy, from all over the world. Recreate these dishes from tested, detailed recipes, for your family and friends.

Faraway Places . . .

Whether it's to remind you of places you've enjoyed visiting, or to learn about places you're still hoping to see, you'll find the travel articles informative and interesting — and just perfect for armchair travelling.

Harlequin

An annual subscription to the magazine — 12 issues — costs just $9.00.

Look for the order form on the next page.

Don't miss your copy of North America's most exciting and enchanting magazine!

Subscribe now to the Harlequin Romance readers' own magazine...Harlequin... available only through Harlequin Reader Service 12 exciting editions for only $9.00